FORGOTTEN PROMISE

FORGOTTEN PROMISE

ARC Shifters

By

Julie Trettel

Forgotten Promise
ARC Shifters: Book Eight

Cover Art by, Logan Keys of Cover of Darkness

Thanks and Acknowledgments

After 27 books published just in this world, I'm not sure who's left that I haven't thanked already. LOL I try to make these personal and meaningful without being too repetitive to those that I constantly cherish and thank for the unconditional love and support they show me.

This time it might seem a little vague, but I have this small group of amazing women (not always exclusively women but was for this one) who supported this book. I dub them my "Cleanup Crew". They've become an integral part of my editing team. They are handpicked for a variety of reasons and vary book to book to read an early copy of the book and provide feedback while hunting for any stingy little errors remaining to ensure I can give you the absolute best story possible. They don't know each other, I work with them one on one, but if it was you, whether for this book or another, thank you. You know who you are!

Tyler
Chapter 1

"Hey Karis, want to go to a movie this weekend?" I asked.

She laughed. "Damon's back in town."

I frowned. He wasn't supposed to be home until Sunday. I'd already bought the tickets.

"So what? We only get to hang out when your mate is gone?"

"You know you aren't exactly his favorite person, right?"

"He's not still mad about that. It was freshman year, you hadn't even met him yet. Plus, he loves me."

"You just like to poke the bear and need to stop."

I knew Damon was listening in and Karis really did know me too well, but she didn't really understand that he and I had a common purpose in life…keeping her safe.

"He's just jealous that you were mine first."

I heard the growl and felt a moment of victory.

"Fine. I'll find another date for the movie."

I was grinning as I waited for it.

"Listen you little shit, you are not dating my mate."

I laughed. "Too easy. Welcome back, Damon. How was Alaska?"

He sighed and I could hear Karis laughing in the background.

"It was fine," he said. "And I'm hanging up now to show my mate exactly how much I missed her while I was gone."

"Gross. You two kids have fun."

I hung up the phone and shook my head.

Damon Rossi had been the biggest playboy on campus when

I arrived at the ARC.

I met Karis Begay my first day at Archibald Reynolds College. She was one of my favorite people in the entire world and my first true friend here. We had dated and things were going well right up until she met Damon.

Boy had she tamed him quickly.

They were true mates and there was no way I would get in the way of that, as if I could even compete against a true mate. That was the most coveted thing in the world for a wolf shifter.

I had bailed out gracefully, but since Damon had threatened to kill me when he became ridiculously territorial of Karis, I'd stuck around and remained her friend, her best friend. Mostly it just irked the future Alpha, but I also knew he would do anything to keep her happy, even putting up with a shit like me.

Despite what it looked and sounded like to others, even Karis at times, Damon and I did have an understanding. I liked to provoke him, but I also respected the bond they had and would never come between it. He knew that.

Lately Damon was spending a lot of time at the Alaskan Pack in preparation to someday take over as Alpha from Karis's grandfather. She was the last of the Begay wolves and her mate was destined to ascend to the highest position in any wolf pack.

If someone had asked me after first meeting Damon whether I thought he would someday be an Alpha, I would have laughed in their face, but being with Karis had changed him. I would never admit it to his face, but he was a really good guy and a great mate. Someday he would be a powerful Alpha too.

I would have made a terrible Alpha. My wolf wasn't strong enough and I had no desire for such responsibility.

She had chosen well, but I would never in a million years admit that to him.

Despite my original thoughts on the guy, he really was one of the good ones.

He was also my fraternity brother. Much to his disgust, at the same time he was wishing he could rip my head off believing I was after his girl, I rushed Delta Omega Gamma.

My brother had been a DOG, so despite Damon's protests, they were required to let me rush as a legacy.

Damon had put up a campaign to keep me out of the

doghouse, but once it came to light why the guy hated me so much, even he had begrudgingly accepted my pledge.

Since Karis was three years younger, Damon had graduated a few years back and had stuck around for her to finish up school. We were seniors now. And since after graduation they would be moving to Alaska, he was having to spend a lot more time up north training.

That was good news for me because I got more time with my friend.

Come to think of it, I'd always gotten along with girls best. Sure, I had my brothers and loved living in the doghouse with them, but the ones I confided in the most had always been girls and right now, that was Karis.

Pete walked into the room we shared. He'd been staying out a lot later lately. I knew something was up with him, but he wasn't the type to share personal stuff until he was ready. I knew better than to even try to push him. It only made him more reclusive every single time.

Pete, Brian, and I had been roommates and friends since freshman year too. I was closer to them than my real biological brother.

We didn't always get along. Brian and I especially fought often. Pete was more like Switzerland of our trio. Still, I would give my life to help either of them and they knew it.

"Whatcha got there?" Pete asked.

I sighed and held up the tickets.

"Thought I'd surprise Karis with that movie she's been wanting to see tomorrow night, but Damon returned."

"Sorry man. Is that the chick flick she's been talking about?"

"Yeah."

"I think that's the one Brian and Amber are looking to go to tomorrow. She has a friend in town visiting and he asked me to double with them. I can't. You should go. I mean you already have the tickets even."

I frowned. "How come he didn't ask me to go?"

"Probably because Damon was supposed to be out of town, and you sort of get lost spending all your time with Karis when that happens. He's still convinced you're pining for her.

I snorted. "I'm not."

"I know that's what you say."

"Pete, I'm not. I love Karis. She's like my best friend, but it's nothing like that."

"You're telling me she's not the girl who got away? Or more like was taken away?"

I laughed. "No, she's not. Look, she's more like a sister to me than anything."

"So you've told us before. It's okay man, there's no judgement here."

I shook my head. "I kissed her when we were dating and even before Damon showed up I knew we were just friends. There was nothing, and I mean *nothing* there. Our wolves hate each other. So seriously, she really is more like the little sister I never had, and I am not pining over her. I just enjoy irritating Rossi."

Pete chuckled. "Okay, now that I believe."

Brian walked in and looked at the two of us.

"Don't you guys have anything better to do on Friday night?"

"Nope," I said.

"Damon came back early," Pete explained.

I groaned. "You need help."

"Yeah, sure, we need help. You hearing this, Pete?" Brian teased.

They both got a good laugh at my expense. I hadn't planned to go out tonight with Karis or anyone else, despite what they thought. The whole party scene had been weighing on me for a while now. It was getting old and felt like a chore dressing up and smiling every weekend.

I was sure my funk had more to do with the fact that I was in my final semester of my senior year and had absolutely no idea what I was going to do with my life once that diploma was in my hands.

I supposed I would go home to New York City and find a job in the financial district with the humans or something. That had always been my plans, but as the days went by I realized I was struggling to submit to a life in the city surrounded by tall buildings, sidewalks, unbearable traffic, and humans.

We had space to run in Central Park, but it wasn't always the safest choice. With each passing year there seemed to be more people around. The tourists were the worst.

I'd gotten spoiled at the ARC. We had woods to run in and open spaces where we didn't have to hide who we were. Growing up in the city I had never had that before, but now I was struggling to go back to living that lie and hiding from everyone I cared about.

The Pack there was large and held plenty of opportunities for pack community, but it was a big city and easy to get lost in. I could feel the walls shrinking in around me just thinking about it.

I realized that while I was heading for my dark place of worries and concerns, Pete and Brian were still talking and now they were staring at me…waiting.

"Uh, what?"

Brian shook his head and smirked. I knew they must have still been talking about Karis.

"I said, if Pete can't go tomorrow, would you want to double date with me and Amber?"

I looked down at the tickets. "*Love Life* at seven?"

"Uh, that's oddly specific."

I held up the tickets. "Was going to surprise Karis because I know Damon hates being dragged to chick flicks and she's been wanting to see it."

"And she ditched you when her mate returned early to surprise her?"

"Pretty much. I can call around. I'm sure I can find a date. Would love to hang out with you two love birds."

Brian and Amber weren't true mates, but you'd never believe that if you were to hang out with them. They were crazy in love, and mostly just crazy. I was happy for my friend. Not everyone had the opportunity to find their one true mate in this big world. Heck, even I would settle for a compatible mate if I truly loved her like he loved Amber.

"No need if you're up for a semi-blind date."

"Define semi-blind? Like you're going to show me a picture of her first so I know what I'm getting myself into?"

"No, like she's out in the common room right now so you can meet her if you want."

"This is the friend visiting Amber that Pete mentioned?"

"Yeah. She's a Virginia wolf. They had mostly grown up together. She's one of Amber's best friends."

"But she doesn't go to school here?"

"Nope. She stayed on the east coast, and I think she already graduated. Amber says she's super smart."

"Great, another nerd?"

Amber was one of the most studious people I knew. I could never understand what she saw in Brian, a guy who could care less about going to classes and believed college was a time for fun before you were forced to grow up. I guess in some ways opposites really did attract.

Brian rolled his eyes. "She's not a nerd."

"You know what I mean."

"Dude, you're one of the smartest guys I know."

"We don't talk about that, remember?"

It was true, numbers just came easy to me, always had. I had changed my major a few times since my arrival at the ARC but finally settled on accounting and finance. It was an easy major for me, and I knew I could go home and take Wall Street by storm.

Just the thought of that seemed to set my wolf on edge.

I didn't want to live my life in a cubicle crunching numbers.

"So are you in or not?" Brian finally asked.

"Yeah, sure. I already have the tickets; they might as well be put to use."

"Do you want to come meet her first? You can always bail if it's not going to be a match. I know you've been overly picky lately with the ladies."

I sighed. "Do I have time for a shower first?"

He looked at his watch. "Yeah, I guess. I'll just give her a tour of the place and we'll be hanging out when you're done."

"Okay. Give me fifteen minutes."

I jumped up and grabbed my toiletry bag, a clean pair of jogging pants, and tee-shirt and headed for the bathroom.

I'd gone to the gym for a workout after classes and knew I wasn't fit to meet someone new who I was potentially going on a double date with the next day.

Hi, I'm Tyler. I know you're a wolf, so don't get close enough to smell me.

I shook my head and stepped into the shower before it even warmed up. The shocking cold cut through my funk faster than anything. I didn't just stand there though, I washed quickly and was out before the water had fully heated.

I shivered, sending droplets of water all over the bathroom.

Knowing Brian was waiting for me, I toweled off and

dressed.

I stopped by my room and dropped off my things then walked into the common room barefoot. Normally I wouldn't dare walk around that place without shoes on, but I knew for a fact the new pledge class had just finished scrubbing the place clean not even an hour ago.

Brian and Amber were sitting on the couch and in the chair facing me was a gorgeous redhead. She looked up and our eyes met.

Mate! my wolf rejoiced in my head.

"Uh, what?" I asked aloud staring at her in shock.

There was a sense of familiarity about her.

She's my mate, of course there is a reason, I berated myself.

I had a million questions I wanted to ask her but instead I stood there frozen like an idiot.

"Tyler? Are you okay?" Amber asked.

I thought I nodded but I really couldn't be sure.

"Tyler!" Brian said, trying to get my attention.

I shook my head. "Uh, yeah. Hi. I'm Tyler."

The look on the girl's face morphed from recognition to shock to pissed in the blink of an eye.

That could not be good.

She stood up and crossed her arms over her chest. Her breasts lifted as if on full display. I couldn't help it. I looked down.

"Seriously?" she asked. "Eyes up here."

I looked up to meet her glare. There was a stubbornness there I wasn't prepared for. It was like a punch in my gut. But there was a hint of pain in her eyes too.

What had I done to piss her off already? I'd only told her my name.

"So, what's your name?" I blurted out and her eyes flashed with hurt and then recovered to anger.

"Nice," she said. "Unbelievable."

She turned to leave.

I crossed the room in record time.

"Wait," I practically begged reaching for her arm.

A jolt of sheer pleasure shot right through me at the contact.

"Please. Just tell me your name."

She pursed her lips.

"Figure it out yourself, Tyler Anthony Nigel Klein."

She turned on her heels and left the house as I stood feeling like I'd just been hit by a semi-truck.

"Tyler? What the hell just happened?" Brian asked.

"I don't know," I admitted.

"I should go check on her. Maybe tomorrow isn't such a good idea," Amber said.

"What? No. I'm in. I already bought the tickets."

"Yeah, but I'm not sure she's actually going to agree to go with you."

"She will. It's all just a big misunderstanding. She took me by surprise, that's all."

"I didn't even realize you two knew each other," Amber said as she walked out the door.

"We don't," I whispered. But the words felt like a lie as they rolled off of my tongue.

Josie

Chapter 2

Oh my gosh! Oh my gosh!

That was Tyler, my Tyler. My wolf wanted to claim him, but he had no idea who I was.

That hurt more than anything. I understood we had been six the last time we saw each other, and we had lost touch over the years, but there was no way I could ever forget the sweet boy who had promised to mate me when his wolf came in. He was my first love, and now here he was in the flesh. He certainly was not the gangly little boy I remembered. He was a hot as sin man now. And he was my one true mate. I knew it with every fiber of my being. But he couldn't even remember my name.

Life hadn't always been easy for me, but Tyler had remained the one constant I held on to, even if there was no way he could possibly understand that.

My parents were nomads who struggled to stay in one place for too long. When I was three we'd settled into New York City. There was a Pack there and I thought we'd stay forever. I'd been allowed to play with the other shifter kids and even go to preschool with them.

That was where I'd met Tyler Klein.

To be honest, I couldn't remember much of my life before Tyler. It was almost as if life had begun with him.

I couldn't tell you the name of any other person from the

New York Pack, but I would never forget him.

He was my first friend, my first skinned knee, my first crush, my first broken bone, my first kiss, my first fight, my first love. Tyler Klein had been my first everything and when he found out my family was moving again, he made me a promise that when his wolf came in, he would find me and make me his mate.

Clearly, he had long since forgotten that, but I never had.

When things had gotten tough, I'd held tight to that promise. I'd stared up at the stars and talked to him when there had been no one else in my life to confide in. I knew he couldn't hear it, but I also never doubted that he was out there, somewhere, staring up at the same night's sky.

To six year old me, Tyler had been my whole world.

To eight year old me, locked in my parents' van while they went dancing at some club in Miami, he had kept me company in the form of a teddy bear I'd named after him to have something tangible to talk to.

To ten year old me, who cried alone in a tent while my parents hunted somewhere in Yellowstone National Park for two weeks, Tyler Teddy had been my lifeline, especially on the stormy nights.

To twelve year old me, when I begged my parents not to move again, he had been there in my heart as a reminder of better times and a promise of better days to come.

To fourteen year old me, Tyler Teddy had stayed by my side as I was sent away to live with my aunt in the Virginia Pack. It had been everything I had asked for, but it was a terrifying time for me because I had never even met Aunt Courtney. Tyler had been there for me then, too, even if only in my own imagination.

When no one asked sixteen year old me to the homecoming dance, I'd staged my own at home in my room with Tyler Teddy. Remembering that somewhere out there was Tyler Klein, that he was going to come for me someday, had gotten me through every bad situation of my life.

At seventeen my wolf came in and I grew up. I'd packed that bear away and hung up the dreams of a child. I was stronger, and I was ready. I graduated high school early and went to college, I moved on and graduated the previous year from nursing school.

I had never really expected to see him again and there was no way he could possibly understand the impact he'd left on my life all those years ago. I wasn't sure I could ever explain that to him. It was embarrassing and pathetic, and I had worked hard the last few years to overcome my childhood. I had roots now and stability. I even had a few friends, like Amber.

It had taken a lot for me to fly across the country to visit her. Sure, it was something I'd wanted to do, but deviating even the smallest bit from my regimented and carefully planned life turned me into that scared little girl. This had been a big step for me, but I had to remind myself over and over again that taking a small vacation before starting a new job was a normal thing to do and did not at all make me anything like my parents and their 'go where the wind leads them' lifestyle.

The shock of seeing him brought it all back almost like cutting open an old wound.

I knew I had no right to be angry at Tyler. It wasn't his fault my life had been shitty. It was a lot of expectation to put on a six year old, yet somehow seeing him standing there now and having no clue who I was when he had been such a prominent part of my life had felt like an arrow had been shot straight through my heart and the bitch of it all was that my wolf made it painfully clear that he was meant to be mine.

I should have been rejoicing in that fact, but all I felt was sad for all the years I'd missed out on with the only person I'd ever let in and truly cared about and he didn't even remember me.

"Josie? Are you okay?" Amber asked.

I had been so lost in my own grief and trying to process old and new emotions threatening to drown me that I hadn't even heard her approach.

"I'm fine," I said with a sigh.

"I take it you know Tyler already?"

"It's stupid. I shouldn't have lashed out at him like that."

"But you do know him?"

"No, but I did when we were kids."

"Well, I guess I'm glad we got this over with tonight at least."

"What do you mean?"

"He was supposed to be your date tomorrow night for the movie."

"What? I thought you said I was going with a Pete."

"Pete apparently has plans and pawned you off on Tyler."

I snorted. "Great. Just great."

"It's fine. He already bought the tickets, but Brian will just buy them off him and we'll go as a girls' night instead."

I felt like an idiot. My emotions were so jacked up that I wasn't thinking straight. This was still my Tyler. Of course I wanted to catch up and know he was doing okay.

Mine, my wolf growled.

And there was that, too.

If he was truly my one true mate, it wasn't like I could just run away and ignore it. I could already feel myself caving and even looking forward to seeing him again.

"You know what? It's okay. You were looking forward to seeing this with Brian and if Tyler already bought my ticket, then let's just go."

She gave me a look like I was insane.

"Are you sure? We got the impression you didn't like him."

There was no way I was ready to explain the depth of emotions I'd felt seeing him after all these years, or the fact that he was my one true mate.

"I was just surprised and didn't handle it well. I'll be more prepared to deal with it next time."

"We don't have to."

"No, a double date sounds like fun, Amber. Really." I linked arms with my closest friend and laid my head on her shoulder. "Thanks for inviting me out here. I've missed you."

"Miss you more."

"Want to go shopping for new dresses tomorrow?"

"Definitely. I booked us a day at the spa, too. Mani pedis?"

"You certainly know the way to my heart."

We both laughed and I felt a little better as we walked back to her room.

Mate, my wolf whined as we walked away from the doghouse.

*****

"Best day ever!" Amber squealed. "I wish you would just

move out here so we could do this more often."

I froze in place. "I, uh…"

"Oh my gosh. Josie, I'm so sorry. I wasn't thinking. I just miss having you around."

I took a deep breath. "I know. It's cool. And if you come back home, I'll be there."

I hadn't confided all the trauma of my childhood to Amber, but she knew or at least suspected enough. I hated moving around and all I'd ever wanted was a place to call home. I'd found that in the Virginia Pack. I had my Aunt Courtney and a few friends. I kept them all at arm's length always protecting my heart. I'd been disappointed too much in my lifetime not to guard myself from letting it happen again.

It might not sound like much to some, but for me it was everything. I was safe and comfortable. I had long ago convinced myself I would never need anything more.

It had been a spur of the moment decision to come to California to visit Amber, a sort of graduation present to myself. It terrified me that I'd up and done it… just like my parents.

I knew I wasn't anything like them. I was responsible and contributed to my Pack. I was everything they weren't, and one special occasion trip was not going to change that.

"Now how does this one look?" Amber asked.

She twirled around in a hot pink dress that showed off her legs and highlighted her short blonde hair.

"Brian isn't going to know what hit him."

"I know, right? Your turn. Try on the red one."

I crinkled my nose. "You know red never looks right on me with my hair."

Instead, I put on the blue one I had eyed on the mannequin in the store front. It was shorter than anything I would typically wear, and it was tighter than my usual choices too. But it made me feel alive and a little sexy.

"Don't freak out. What about this one?"

I stepped out of the dressing room and turned in a circle for her to see it all.

Her jaw dropped. "Yes!"

"Amber, I'm being serious."

"Me too. It is the perfect color and makes your eyes just pop.

And girl, your boobs are hot!"

I laughed. "You act like you've never seen them before."

"Certainly not on full display like that."

I blushed and immediately started second guessing the choice.

"No, no, no. You're wearing it. And I'm buying it for you to make damn sure you do."

"How is your buying it going to ensure I wear it?"

"Pure and simple—guilt."

I laughed. "You're insane, you know that right?"

"But you love me anyway."

"Yes, I do."

"Let's check out and grab some ice cream before we hit the salon."

"Sounds perfect."

Ice cream, manicures, pedicures, and we even splurged to have our hair and makeup professionally done. It was nice to feel pampered. I'd never really done anything like it before having avoided school formals and any other opportunity to do something so frivolous. I had no idea it would be so much fun.

By the time we were heading back to Amber's room, my nerves were starting to grow. I knew I looked hot in the new dress but wasn't sure I'd have the guts to wear it. Was I trying to punish myself or Tyler with that thing?

"Oh no," I said.

"What?"

"I don't have any shoes to wear with that dress."

Amber laughed. "Girl, relax and just be yourself tonight."

I grinned. "You're saying wear my Van's?"

"It's so you and I promise your feet are the last thing Tyler's going to be looking at so why not just be comfortable?"

"Are you sure?"

"I'm sure." She grinned, before pausing and grabbing my arm. "Wait! Are we trying to get Tyler, punish Tyler, or just make him trip over his tongue and slip on his own drool?"

I laughed. "I have no idea."

I was pretty sure I was still in shock from seeing him. I hadn't even begun to process the whole true mate thing and I had failed to mention that part to Amber. She was a romantic at heart who lived for a good fairytale and finding one's true mate always seemed like the sweetest kind of fairytale for a shifter.

I was a little surprised that she wasn't planning on waiting for her own true mate. She had confided in me that she and Brian were talking about petitioning their Packs for permission to be compatible mates.

It had always seemed like a stupid, archaic process to me. Why would anyone need permission to mate? To me it should be like human marriages. I can see notifying the Packs, but seeking permission was ridiculous.

Of course, my personal fairytale had never once included a true mate. I had always held close to my heart that I would someday mate Tyler. It was literally my childhood dream that I never actually believed could come true. Though, it had gotten me through a lot of crap in life believing that someone somewhere out there was mine and that he actually cared about me.

I realized how stupid that was as I grew up and reality had hit, yet when I'd had the opportunities to date, I'd always said no. Amber knew that which is probably why she was planning to catch me off-guard with a blind date.

Of course, my perfect fairytale had never ended with Tyler as my true mate. I'd always assumed we'd just be compatible mates.

I'd dreamed a thousand times what it would be like to see him again. I'd wondered what he would look like. Well, I knew that now and he was way out of my league. I always remembered him as cute, and so then as my teenage self the adult fantasies matured, so did he. But my imagination hadn't done him justice because that man was far above anything I could have imagined. He was smoking hot. How was it that he was even single and available for a double date with a stranger?

Was that what I was to him? A stranger? Because he didn't feel like a stranger to me.

Maybe if I'd just told him who I was then he would remember, but my pride, and my heart couldn't risk it, because what if he still didn't remember me?

Tyler

Chapter 3

It had taken everything in my power not to run after her, but Brian had stopped me.

"Amber's got it. She'll be fine."

But he didn't understand. That was my mate and I'd seen the hurt I'd caused her. I didn't even understand why.

She had known my name, my full name. That wasn't something I'd just tell a random hook up, besides, my wolf would have known sooner that we'd found our mate and I was certain that was the first time either of us saw her.

"Anthony Nigel? You have two middle names? Wait, your parents gave you the initials TANK? How have I never known this?"

I groaned. My mother had a thing for acronyms. It was how my brother Richard had been saddled with the nickname ROCK – Richard Osiris Christian Klein. But unlike me, he'd owned it and loved the name and attention it brought him.

I'd had to live with being called TANK most of my life. When I came to the ARC, I didn't bring it with me. I'd left it in New York and never looked back.

"Don't. Just don't," I said. "How the hell did she know that?"

"Well clearly there's something there. I mean I'm supposed to be one of your best friends and even I didn't know about the TANK thing."

"Never mention it again, please."

"Okay, okay. Well, no, actually, I gotta tell Pete."

"Brian!" I yelled, trying to intercept him as he headed for our room.

I lunged and tackled him around the ankles. Then I sat on him, pinning him to the floor.

"Swear to me you will never mention this to anyone. Swear it!"

He was laughing when Chad walked in. I looked up at him with a scowl.

"What are you doing here? You don't even live here anymore," I barked.

He just shook his head.

Brian used my distraction to flip me over and pin me to the floor instead.

"So this is how we treat our President these days? Back in my day we showed a lot more respect," Chad said.

I snorted. "Yeah 'back in your day'. You just gave up the position last semester and you still haven't graduated," I reminded him.

Chad shrugged. "It's called a Masters. And last I checked I was still a brother here. I can hang out if I want."

"Yeah, I know. Sorry. It's been a weird night," I conceded.

He stared down at us and chuckled. "I can see that."

"Did you need anything?"

"Nah. I was just stopping in to see if anything was going on. This place is dead tonight when you two are the life of the house."

"Party at Theta house," I informed him.

"And you're not there?"

"Nope, haven't been in the mood."

"He thought he had Karis for the weekend," Brian told him.

Chad nodded. "Yeah, I heard Damon came home early, but obviously he's a little busy today."

"Where's Ember?" It wasn't like the guy didn't have a mate of his own.

"She's in San Marco visiting her sister."

"Oh yeah, I heard about that."

"Not surprised. It did make headlines."

Ember's mom was like top elite in Hollywood. Her family was always on the cover of some magazine or another. Recently she'd gotten the shock of her life discovering her father had an illegitimate daughter that no one knew about…not even him.

And I thought my family had issues.

"Well, you're welcome to hang out here. The twins and Tim won't last long. I'm actually surprised they aren't back yet. Jess and Marie declared it a girls' night and ditched them. They went over to Theta about an hour ago, but you know those two hate going without their ladies."

Chad flopped down on the couch and picked up a controller as he turned the TV on.

It wasn't long before Jackson and Tobi showed up. I swore they had some weird superpower to know exactly when someone was starting up a game on the Xbox.

Like a lot of the brothers, Jackson was sticking around for his Masters, too. It was like the original regime of our brotherhood had moved on, and yet they couldn't seem to actually leave. In Jackson's case, his mate, Tobi, was graduating with me in the spring. He'd worked double time taking year round classes to finish his Masters early.

They were going to be moving back to Tobi's tiny Pack in Canada this summer. Jackson already had a job lined up and had been busy starting a company of his own. It was nice to see the guys hanging around again. I was going to miss my fraternity brothers more than anything when it was time to leave this place.

Kian, our lone panther brother, walked out of his room and looked down at the two of us still wrestling on the floor.

"I don't even want to know," he said.

"Hey man, Chad's just firing up a game and we could use a fourth," Jackson said.

"Yeah, sure."

He looked down at us again as if we were crazy, then stepped over our bodies and joined the others.

I stopped fighting long enough for him to pass, but Brian used it to his advantage and jumped up to run down the hall.

"No!" I yelled.

"They were like that when I got here. I don't want to know either," Chad told them.

"Good thing the pledges cleaned today," Kian said laughing.

"Gross," Tobi said. "You still couldn't pay me to lay on that floor. I've seen it after a party and that cannot be unseen. Now come on. Are you three ready to lose to a girl?"

I laughed as I followed after Brian to the room the three of us shared.

When I was voted in as President of our Delta Omega Gamma chapter, it came with a significant room upgrade, but Brian, Pete, and I had been rooming together since freshman year. I couldn't imagine not having those guys around and up in my space like that.

So, my room sat mostly empty. Brian used it the most when Amber stayed over. Otherwise visiting former brothers would stay there, but I had said no to random hookups. I could still move over at any time, I just didn't see the point. We'd be graduating in a few short months and then this would all be gone for me.

It was a surreal thought.

When I walked back into our room, Brian was already telling Pete about my unfortunate initials.

Pete shrugged like it was no big deal. "I like Tyler better. It's more fitting for you."

"Thank you," I said.

"Are you going to pout now?" Brian teased. "Pete doesn't even care."

"No. I'm just thinking about the girl again. What did you say her name was?"

"Hmm, I didn't."

"Don't be an ass, Brian. What's her name?" I had to know.

"I feel like this is something you should figure out on your own along with why the hell she recognized you and then ran away upset."

It felt like he'd just lodged a knife straight through my heart. She had been upset. Inside that stubborn exterior, I'd seen it in her eyes.

Mate, my wolf growled making it clear he was upset I hadn't gone after her.

"Wait, a girl ran away from you? Was this Amber's friend?" Pete asked.

"Yup. She was upset but also pissed. There's a story there, our boy just isn't confessing to it."

"Because I legitimately do not know, you guys. I promise

you I've never seen her before." Again, this felt like a lie, but for the life of me I couldn't place why.

It was like it was there on the edges of my memory, but I couldn't get past the part of her being my true mate.

I should have just told Brian that from the start, but I couldn't seem to form the words.

"I'm going to go for a walk," I said.

"Don't bother. Amber already texted me and they are in for the night."

I groaned. Why did my friends have to know me so well?

"Tell me her name!"

"No."

"Come on Brian, just tell him."

"Let me think about it… no."

"You really are an ass," I said, rolling over so my back was towards them.

I knew it was going to be a long night. In my memory I couldn't quite place that face, but yet, I knew those eyes.

Much to my shock, I did go to sleep eventually, and I dreamed of younger easier times and the only redhead I'd ever known—Josie.

I broke out into a cold sweat and jumped from my bed.

No, it couldn't be.

I tried to reconcile the gorgeous ginger with my first true friend. We had been so young and Josie had been a freckled faced little girl. It wasn't possible, yet it was those damned eyes. *Dark blue like the ocean waters.*

Josie had been my first real friend, and probably why I'd always befriended girls, but her family had moved when we were just kids and I'd never heard from her again. I had no idea what happened to that little girl. The red hair and blue eyes were similar, but I still struggled to reconcile the two.

I tossed and turned the rest of the night almost waking Brian up to confirm it. Could that really be little Josie all grown up?

I couldn't get the thought out of my mind and my wolf was going insane. I finally gave up just before sunrise and took off for the woods.

I needed to run.

The problem with this plan was that my wolf only wanted to

run to her. It took a lot of effort to keep that from happening.

I needed to be patient, that was all.

I'd find out if my suspicions were right soon enough.

I grabbed some breakfast and headed back to the house.

Brian was on the phone with Amber and I overheard enough to know the girls had a big pampering day ahead of them.

I considered what I should wear. Then berated myself for stressing over it. I'd never given much thought to such things. I'd made such a terrible first impression though that I didn't want to screw things up with her again.

I mentally went through my wardrobe in my head settling on a blue polo and khakis. I knew without a doubt the color would make my blond hair and blue eyes stand out. I needed to look my best as a distraction to get her to even talk to me again.

The day had passed like I was stuck in my own personal hell. I didn't think it could possibly go any slower. Then suddenly it was time to leave to pick up the girls.

I knew I would get on my knees and grovel if necessary, but hoped it wouldn't come down to that.

I needed a second chance and this semi-blind date was it.

The pressure of knowing I might not get another opportunity to make things right terrified me. I couldn't lose this girl. If she disappeared on me, I knew I would spend the rest of my life pining for her. Now that I'd caught her scent and knew who she was to me, I couldn't let her just walk away ever again. Watching her run out the door already felt like the biggest mistake of my life.

Josie

Chapter 4

I couldn't stop fidgeting with the hem of my dress. It was so short. What was I thinking?

"You look nice. Stop messing with it," Amber scolded.

I liked her all dressed up in her pink gown. She looked far more sophisticated than I did. I suddenly felt like a little girl playing dress up next to her.

"You do too. Do you think I should change into a pair of your dress shoes though?"

"It's just a movie, Josie. And you look amazing. Just relax. Tyler's always fun to hang out with. I'm sure whatever was up with you two last night will work itself out. Tonight is all about fun."

"Do you think they'll even dress up?"

"Of course."

"But how can you be certain?"

"Because I texted Brian this morning and told him to."

"Okay, maybe I won't feel quite as awkward about this dress then."

"Are you kidding? You look hot, Josie. Tyler won't be able to take his eyes off of you. But if he lays a hand on you or makes you uncomfortable, just say the word and I will neuter him."

I groaned. "I don't think that will be necessary."

"I'm just saying. Okay, I think they're here. Get your sexy ass out that door. Our dates have arrived."

"Shouldn't we wait for them to actually knock?"

"Nah. They're walking up now, let's go. Brian hasn't gotten our tickets yet, so while you and Tyler are fine, I'm worried he may have screwed us."

"Do you really think it'll be that busy?"

She shrugged. "Hard to tell. It is Saturday night, big date night."

"Yeah, I guess," I said, not that I would know since I'd never really been on an actual date before.

I was pretty sure that was the real reason why Amber was rushing me out before the guys arrived. If they were there and I freaked out like I had last night, I knew she feared I would refuse to go and feel obligated to stay home with me.

I wiped my sweating hands on the hem of my dress. I couldn't remember ever being this nervous about anything in my entire life. What if he didn't show up? What if I'd made such a fool of myself that he was upset and refused to give me a second chance? Surely, he felt the mating call as strongly as I had. I'd seen the fear in his eyes, so I knew he must have.

We met them in the stairwell.

Brian let out a low whistle and then pulled Amber into his arms for a kiss.

"Babe, we were just coming up to get you," he told her.

"Don't want to be late," Amber lied. This time I could hear it in her voice. She was worried I'd freak out and bail on this date.

They descended the stairs while Tyler stood there staring at me. His jaw dropped and I was pretty sure his eyes nearly bugged out of their sockets too.

"Hi," he said.

"Hi."

I tried to remember to breathe.

"Wow, you look stunning." He looked down and grinned. I thought he even relaxed just a little. "Nice shoes."

My cheeks burned.

"Thanks," I mumbled noticing his blue polo matched my dress to perfection. "It almost looks like we coordinated on purpose."

He looked down and chuckled. "I guess it does."

"Did you bring the tickets?" I wanted to turn and run back. I was in over my head and asking stupid questions.

He grinned and then checked his back pocket holding them up.

"All set. Shall we?"

He offered me his arm. I looked at it and then back up at him. His face fell and he motioned for me to go ahead of him instead.

It had been almost twenty-four hours since I ran out on him and left him standing there in shock. The pain was still fresh, but I pushed it out of my head. If I were going to get to know this Tyler, I couldn't keep holding the past over him. He wasn't even aware we had a past. It was ridiculous.

I made a vow to push my fears aside and try to actually enjoy the night.

As walked outside and the chill of the night air hit me, I shivered. Tyler placed his hand at the base of my spine to guide me towards the car. His sharp intake of breath told me he felt the electricity coursing between us too.

The little jolts of pleasure that his touch shot through me were a bit unnerving and made me jumpy.

Amber and Brian carried the conversation as we rode to the theater together. They were sitting in the front seat while we were in the back.

I caught Tyler staring at me on more than one occasion. His eyes were searching mine like he was looking for answers probably for why I had freaked out and run out on him the night before. He looked more curious now than concerned. I couldn't help but watch him, too.

The feelings welling up in me were powerful and left me with a heady feeling. It was almost like I imagined being high would feel, which was funny as it was something I'd never done before. I know people who were addicted to it though, and I understood, but I thought I could easily become addicted to the sensations he was causing me just from his close proximity.

It should have felt awkward, yet somehow it didn't.

I stole another glance at him. It was hard to believe this was really my Tyler.

When we got to the theater, He turned to me. "Would you like some popcorn or a drink, Josie?"

My jaw dropped and my heart pounded. He'd called me by

my name.

Amber smacked Brian.

"You promised not to tell him. I wanted to see him squirm a little longer."

"I swear, I didn't."

"He didn't," Tyler confirmed, never taking his eyes off me.

The relief I felt was overwhelming. He remembered me.

He offered me his arm again. This time I took it even welcoming the shockwaves that wracked through my body at his touch.

I beamed up at him, and my heart sort of flipped in my chest.

I was in way over my head with this guy.

"So, Josie, popcorn?"

I loved hearing my name roll off of his tongue with ease.

"Sure."

"Butter?"

"Always," I said with a laugh.

"Drink?"

I sighed.

"What?"

"Nothing. A Coke is fine."

"Uh-uh, what is it?"

"I just hate how expensive everything is at concessions here," I admitted.

I couldn't help it. I hadn't always had enough and learned at a young age to conserve everything I could. I hated being wasteful and I knew there was no way I was going to drink an entire drink by myself.

"My treat," he reminded me.

"I know," I sighed.

"So what would you do normally?"

"Kiddie tray, ask for a cup for water, or if it were with someone I could share with, I would."

"So, a cheap date," he teased.

I blushed and shrugged.

"Frugal then," he corrected.

"What can I get you two?" the guy behind the counter asked.

"Large popcorn, large Coke," he said and then winked at me as he grabbed two straws.

"You didn't have to do that," I told him after we got our stuff and started to make our way into the theater.

He shrugged. "I don't mind at all."

"Josie, Tyler, over here," Amber yelled across the room when we walked into the theater.

Tyler shot me an apologetic look as we walked over to join them. He and Brian took the ends so Amber and I could sit together. With the popcorn and drink between us, the room darkened, and the movie started.

I couldn't seem to stop jumping every time our arms brushed. It was like I knew it was coming, but I still wasn't quite prepared for it. Every single time.

When we both reached for popcorn at the same time and our hands touched, I jumped so bad I nearly knocked the bucket from his hands.

I wanted him to touch me though. I was already craving it and looking forward to the next jolt of energy coming from him, yet I still jumped like an idiot. The anticipation alone had my nerves on edge.

I wished I could calm down, but I was still nervous.

This was Tyler Klein, I shouldn't be nervous around him. When we were kids I could tell him anything and he always seemed to know what to say to make everything better. He had known how to pull me out of my shell and bring messy chaos to my life and somehow make it feel okay.

I wanted him to make this better too, but I also wasn't ready to confide things in him the way I had as a child. And I didn't like messy chaos anymore. I liked order and structure. I craved it. I needed it.

I looked over and saw Amber sniff. I grabbed a napkin and passed it to her.

"Thanks."

I smiled feeling a little more like myself, but also realizing I had no clue what was happening in the movie. It didn't look very good anyway. The previews made it seem much better than it actually was.

While my guard was down, Tyler reached over and took my hand linking our fingers together. I didn't jump this time as I stared at our connected hands and felt this sudden calm wash over me as if everything was going to be alright.

I looked up at him and he gave me a crooked smile.

My heart did a flip in my chest once more and I settled down to try and salvage whatever was left of the movie.

In that moment, I felt like maybe I could do this, and everything was going to be okay.

Tyler

Chapter 5

Josie was very anxious, that much was clear.

I wanted to reach over and take her hand sooner, but I thought she might freak out even more, so I had kept my hands to myself which wasn't an easy thing to do when all I wanted was to touch her.

When I couldn't take it anymore, I reached for her, lacing our fingers together. Much to my surprise, she relaxed. She even smiled at me before tuning into the movie which I was certain she didn't have a clue what the thing was even about.

I watched enough of it to know it was fine, maybe a little boring. Certainly nothing spectacular.

My phone beeped towards the end. I grabbed it quickly to silence it.

KARIS: Still up for that movie.

ME: You missed it. And it sucks ass. You can thank me later.

KARIS: You went without me. *pout*

I shook my head and grinned.

Popcorn pelted the side of my face.

"Ow. What the hell?" I whisper yelled.

"Are you seriously texting her while you're out on a date, Tyler?" Brian asked.

I frowned and flicked him the bird.

ME: Gotta go. Brian's being an ass.

KARIS: LOL You took Brian in my place?

ME: Double date. Wish me luck.

KARIS: Call me tonight, or tomorrow. Want to hear everything.

I put my phone away with a shake of my head. She was never going to believe this.

Josie was watching me. I looked up and caught her eye for only a second as she quickly looked back to the movie screen, but I didn't miss that bit of hurt there.

I sighed. I knew from watching my brothers fall to their mates that this wasn't going to be easy, but it killed me to know I had hurt her even in some small way.

I gave her hand a squeeze. I needed her to know that I was here, and I wasn't going anywhere. She was my mate. Why would she feel threatened by me texting someone?

I would never really understand women.

She hadn't jumped out of her seat and run for the door when I squeezed her hand, so maybe I just misread the look in her eyes.

We rode out the rest of the movie. I got up and stretched missing her touch the second she removed her hand from mine.

"I booked us a table for dinner. You two up for it?" Brian asked.

Josie started to make an excuse to bail, but Amber cut her off leaving no room for negotiation. All I heard was that she wanted to get away from me and my wolf was pissed at me for screwing things up and hurting our mate once again.

I felt like I couldn't win.

When Brian pulled up in front of the fancy steakhouse that Damon worked at I groaned.

At least he was home with Karis. Then it dawned on me that she had asked if I still wanted to see the movie tonight. That meant one of two things: they were either fighting, which never happened, or…

"Seat them in my section," Damon told the hostess before winking at me.

"Shit!"

Brian chuckled then tried to cover it by clearing his throat.

"I thought you said he was home with Karis tonight," he said, trying to look innocent.

"You just had to pick this place." I shook my head.

"It's the nicest place in town. What do you want from me?"

"Is everything okay?" Josie asked.

I sighed.

"Yup. This could be entertaining at least," Brian said.

I groaned as I escorted her to our table.

Damon came right over the second we were seated.

"Can I get you guys something to drink while you look over the menus? Perhaps a cherry Coke? We have fresh cherries at the bar."

He grinned down at me as I shot him a look.

Josie shook her head. "Tyler's allergic to cherries."

I grinned. "I can't believe you remember that."

She shrugged like it was no big deal. "I remember a lot of things," she mumbled, warming me from the inside.

"Hmm. I know you. I know you, and, *unfortunately*, I know you," Damon said pointing to me. "But I definitely do not know you. Hi, I'm Damon."

She smiled politely and nodded while otherwise ignoring him.

I grinned and shrugged. "You're losing your touch with the ladies, Damon."

I knew the second the words slipped out that it had been a mistake.

He squatted down to ensure he had her full attention. "Let me try again. Hi, I'm Damon Rossi and you are way out of his league. Wow. You are absolutely stunning."

Josie blushed.

And then Damon reached for her hand and brought it to his lips, kissing the back of it.

I knew he was just torturing me.

I knew I shouldn't react.

A growl slipped out in warning, and I started to shake all over.

Mate! my wolf growled angrily in my head.

Damon's eyes widened as he dropped her hand and slowly stood.

Josie's head whipped around to me. I could feel fur sprouting on my hands.

"I didn't know," Damon insisted. "Shit!"

Josie reached over and placed her hand on my leg. "Not here," she whispered.

My whole body shuddered, and I regained control over my wolf, but it had shaken me to my very core. I'd never lost it like that. What was happening to me?

"I didn't know," Damon said.

I shot him a look. It shouldn't have mattered if he'd known or not. But then I remembered how much crap I'd given him over the years. I'd been rather kind during his mating period, but I'd enjoyed harassing him more and more over the years.

"Know what?" Amber asked.

"Nothing," Josie and I said in unison.

"Uh, okay. Well are you going to order or not?"

"Just water," Josie said.

I nodded to Damon who kept staring at us both with a weird look on his face.

"Damon?" I finally said.

"What? Oh, water, yeah, you got it. What are you having?"

"Water's fine," I said.

Once he had Brian and Amber's order he leaned down and whispered, "Does Karis know?"

I scowled. "Despite what you all seem to think, I do not tell *your* mate everything."

I exaggerated the "your" part for Josie's benefit. I knew everyone thought I had this weird obsession with Karis. I didn't, but I also never gave a shit what others thought about it.

I cared what Josie thought and I didn't want her getting the wrong idea.

Brian snorted. "Sure. You tell Karis literally everything."

Damon shot him a look but didn't join in for once. I almost missed his shitty comebacks.

"I'll be back with your drinks."

He left us and Brian's jaw dropped.

"I've never seen him just walk away from an opening like that." Then he turned to me with worry written all over his face. "Hey man, is everything okay with you and Karis?"

"What? Yeah. Why?"

"I don't know. You and Damon are just acting weird

tonight."

"Uh, okay. Whatever."

Josie was staying very quiet, but every now and then she'd steal a look at me.

"Everything's good here," I told her, breaking whatever awkwardness was setting in around us and wishing we weren't on a double date.

My knee brushed against hers and she jumped again. It felt like I'd just taken another giant step backwards.

"Um, thanks, that's good to know," she said.

"Anything in particular sound interesting?" I asked, trying to keep things as nice and polite as possible.

I just needed to get through this meal and then we could ditch Brian and Amber and maybe really talk about what was happening between us.

Secrets never stayed secret long around the doghouse, so I didn't much care if Brian caught on, but I was pretty certain that Josie hadn't told Amber and I didn't know how she felt about her finding out that we were true mates.

I hated the thought that it might embarrass or bother her in some way.

Then there was also the part about this being my childhood friend, Josie, lingering in the air between us. We needed to talk about that too.

"To be honest, I'm not really hungry after all that popcorn," she finally said.

I relaxed a little and smiled. "Me neither," I confessed. "Want to share something or ditch out and forget it?"

She bit her lip. "You wouldn't mind sharing?"

"Not with you," I said in a softer voice that made her blush. I grinned. "What did you have in mind?"

She shrugged. "Ravioli?"

Damon had just returned with our drinks and jumped right into our conversation.

"Great choice. It's one of my personal favorites."

He winked at me, but I just rolled my eyes.

"So, ravioli for the lady, how about you, Tyler?"

My head whipped back to him. "Tyler?"

"I'm trying to be nice here in hopes you'll leave me a nice fat tip to take *my* girl out to see that movie she's been dying to see."

I laughed. "Don't bother. I already warned her it sucked."

"Didn't you just see it?"

I shrugged "Yeah."

"When did you have time to talk to her?"

"She texted him during the movie," Brian told him.

Damon groaned.

"You have serious issues, man."

"What? She texted me."

"You don't answer her while on a date with…" he froze probably seeing the color drain from Josie at the thought he was about to say "your mate". Instead, he amended himself, "someone else."

I laughed. "You do know she texts me while you two are out all the time."

Damon growled at me and for the first time since we walked into the place, I felt just a little bit normal.

I grinned.

"Asshole," he muttered.

Josie's head whipped around to see how I'd respond, but I just grinned and winked at him.

We made it through the meal with no further issues.

After we paid the bill and were getting ready to leave, Damon stopped back by our table. Brian and Amber had already gotten up and were moving to the door.

He slid in the seat Amber had just vacated and Josie stopped and waited to see what would happen next.

"Okay, cards on the table. I know I give you shit all the time, mostly because you're an asshole. No offense," he told Josie. "It's not personal. He and I have a unique history."

I laughed. "Is that what you call it?"

Damon genuinely smiled and shrugged.

He seemed torn on what to say next but turned to talk to Josie. "Look, in truth, I know Tyler's one of the good guys, not that I will ever admit to this conversation or repeat that again. Don't let the idiot things others say come between you two. I know a mating bond when I see one, and I know what that feels like." He looked right at me. "You gracefully stepped aside for me, and despite the shit I dish out, and your incessant need to stick around like an annoying gnat,

I've always appreciated that. You're not going to get any added stress from me. Mating sucks bad enough on its own."

"Too bad. When you called me an asshole, I felt like the world had righted itself once more."

He chuckled and shook his head. "You're an idiot."

As we stood up Damon shook my hand and then pulled me in for a hug.

"I really am happy for you. I hope you two work things out and are as happy as my mate and I are. Really."

"Uh, thanks, D. I really appreciate that."

Josie's cheeks were on fire.

"Was it really that noticeable?" she blurted out.

"Clearly not to Tweedledee and Tweedledum over there, but I know Tyler well enough to know there's only one reason ever that he would growl at me like that."

She looked at me and sighed.

"It's going to be okay, Josie," I told her. "We have a lot of catching up to do."

"If that's the case, why don't you ditch those two."

"Rode over together and not planning to walk back to campus," I explained.

He tossed me his keys. "Go on, get out of here."

"Why are you being cool about this? You're freaking me out," I confessed.

He grinned. "Oh, well we can't have that, now can we?"

Before I could stop him, Damon reached out and pulled Josie into his arms and rubbed his scent on her.

A ferocious growl escaped me loud enough to cause a nearby table to look our way.

"Get him out of here, quickly," he whispered to Josie. "Payback's a bitch, Tyler."

I could still hear him laughing as Josie dragged me outside.

Josie

Chapter 6

Tyler seemed to relax a little from my touch. It was kind of surreal.

I had no idea what was going on between those two but there was clearly a lot of history there. A few things Tyler had said made me think he really did remember our time together.

"Didn't think you guys were ever coming out of there. What did Damon want?" Brian asked.

"Trouble," I said.

I knew that wasn't entirely true though. I mean the guy had given us his keys so we could be alone. I was nervous at the thought, but I wanted it more than anything.

Tyler ran his hand up and down my spine causing me to shiver.

"It's going to be fine. Look, can Josie and I ditch you two? We have a lot of catching up to do. What, like fifteen, sixteen or so years."

He really knew. No one had to tell him my name and they certainly couldn't have told him when I'd last seen him. He remembered me.

I was taken by surprise just how much that meant to me.

Mine! my wolf demanded, but I was too happy to pay her much attention.

In my heart, Tyler had always been mine.

"When did you really figure it out?"

He shrugged. "I don't know. I'm still having a hard time believing it's really you."

"So you two really do know each other?" Brian asked.

"Sorta. At least we did when we were little. She lived in New York for a few years and then her family up and moved."

I sighed. "They did that a lot."

He held up the keys Damon had given him. "Swiped these off Damon. We're going to ditch the two of you now. Have a good night."

Amber's jaw dropped, but she gave me a thumb's up making my cheeks burn.

She was always trying to get me to go out and be more spontaneous, no doubt she was thinking all that badgering over the years was finally paying off.

The awful thing about being a redhead was that even the slightest bit of embarrassment lit my face every single time. My cheeks were certainly burning bright as I turned to follow Tyler through the parking lot.

"That's my boy!" Brian yelled.

Amber smacked him. "That's my friend."

I tuned them both out and let Tyler lead to me to the car and help me into the passenger seat. Once he was settled, he picked up his phone and dialed a number putting it on speaker phone so that his hands were free, and then he started the car and drove off.

It rang twice and a girl picked up.

My eyes widened and I glared at him.

He gave me a sheepish look.

"Hey Kare, I only have a minute, but Damon needs you to pick him up from work tonight."

"Hello to you, too. He drove himself. He's fine. And why are you calling me? I thought you were on a double date."

"Nah, we ditched Brian and Amber, hence why you need to pick up your mate."

"So, you're on a date and calling me? Are you insane?"

He laughed easily, but I was thinking the same thing. My wolf was on edge and didn't like this one bit.

"Karis, say hi to Josie. Josie, this is Karis, Damon's mate."

"Hello, best friend here. I don't know a Josie," she said.

"I'm just visiting."

"Oh, well, hi. You've got one of the best with you tonight."

I looked over at Tyler. "I know," I said softly.

"Well, have fun and thanks for letting me know. I'll be there on time."

"Oh, don't get carried away. You can let him suffer for a while."

"You'd like that too much. Go enjoy the rest of your date."

She hung up.

I didn't know what to think. I had once been his best friend. Irrationally I felt hurt that he had found another female best friend. It was ridiculous, even I knew that, but everything seemed to be heightened when I was around Tyler, including my lack of rational thoughts.

Was this normal?

Was this the mating call people talked about?

I had heard it made people crazy, but this seemed like a lot.

He didn't seem to be affected at all by me or the mating call, and yet when he'd nearly shifted right there in the middle of the restaurant, my touch had calmed him. That had to mean something, right?

He hadn't denied it when his friend had called him out on it either. That had felt good.

I sniffed and scrunched up my nose, unable to believe that guy had put his scent on me like that. It had happened so quickly that I didn't even think to slap him until he was already walking away. I think I was in shock or something. I wasn't used to random guys hugging me like that. Heck, I wasn't used to anyone touching me, which was probably why Tyler's touches seemed so much more potent than they should have.

"Where are we?" I finally asked as Tyler pulled into a parking lot.

"Back at the doghouse."

"Okay."

I had no idea what to expect or even what to say to him.

He took my hand as we walked up to the house. I stopped on the front porch and turned to him.

"Tyler, maybe this isn't such a good idea. It's been a long day. Maybe we should just say goodnight."

"No," he said leaving no room for argument.

"No?"

"No. We need to talk about what's happening here, Josie."

I gulped. "What exactly is happening here?"

He looked as confused as I felt and didn't seem to have an answer to that.

"I can't think while you smell like him. First things first. You're taking a shower and burning that dress."

"What?" I asked. "I just bought this dress."

"And you look sexy as hell in it, but not while it smells like him."

I wrapped my arms over my chest. "You're not destroying my dress."

He took a step towards me, and I took two steps back.

"I'm not joking here, Josie. He did it on purpose too."

"Because you're after his mate?" I blurted out. I'd heard enough and read the innuendos that everyone was trying to warn me about.

He laughed and he sounded a little crazy. I could feel his wolf's aggression rising.

"I'll explain it later, but first, you're getting out of that dress and washing his scent off of you."

I huffed ready to stand my ground, but he didn't wait for me to argue.

Tyler picked me up and threw me over his shoulder then kicked the front door open and walked down the hall.

A few catcalls rang out in the room we walked through, and my cheeks burned again.

"Tyler, put me down." I protested smacking him on the butt.

My hand stung. Damn, he had a tight ass.

"What are you doing?" Jackson asked.

Tyler growled at him as we walked through to the hallway.

"Tyler, stop acting like a caveman," I squealed causing laughter to erupt from the room we'd just left.

He walked to the door at the end of the hall and set me down once inside.

I crossed my arms over my chest and gave him a stern look.

His eyes lowered to stare at my chest. It took a lot for me not to cover myself.

"Shower, now," he ordered.

"I don't remember you being so bossy."

"I don't remember you reeking of another male. I'm serious, Josie."

"Gah!" I threw my hands up in the air and stomped into the bathroom. A few minutes later he opened the door just as I was about to step into the shower.

I squealed and nearly tripped over the side of the tub.

He kept his eyes on mine as he handed me some soap, shampoo, and conditioner. He also laid out a new toothbrush, toothpaste, and comb by the sink and set out a stack of clothes.

"Thanks," I mumbled.

"Shower," he demanded.

Before he turned to leave, his eyes swept down my naked body and he gave a low growl of appreciation.

It heated up my body from the inside out until I feared I'd combust.

I took a quick and quite cold shower, but when I stepped out, my dress was gone.

"Tyler! Tell me you didn't burn it," I yelled.

All I heard was a chuckle.

I brushed my teeth, combed my hair, and changed into a pair of gym shorts too big for me, but at least it had a drawstring to tighten down enough. It felt weird wearing them when I had no underwear to put on. He must have taken those with the dress.

The shirt was easily two sizes too big, and I was swimming in it.

I stared in the mirror and pouted.

My face had been scrubbed clean and my freckles were more evident.

I looked like a little kid. Gone was the sophisticated woman I had felt I was in that beautiful dress.

I huffed.

There was nothing I could do about that now.

I sniffed the shirt and grinned. He had given me his clothes.

Tyler was trying to cover me in his scent. My heart melted a little.

I pushed aside my aggravation with him and stepped back out into the bedroom.

Tyler was changing the sheets on the bed.

I gulped hard.

"What are you doing?" I asked trying not to freak out a little. This was all new territory for me. I wasn't the girl who was used to being alone with a guy, especially not in his bedroom.

"Almost done. Brian and Amber stay over here sometimes. My wolf is already on edge enough. I can't handle any other males or their scents near you right now."

"That guy that hugged me, Damon, he knew what he was doing, didn't he?"

Tyler sighed as he opened the door and threw the old sheets out into the hallway.

"Yes, he knew exactly what he was doing."

"Why did he do it?"

"Probably thought he was helping in some sick way, but also as payback."

"For what?"

"Hold on," he walked over and pulled me into his arms.

My mouth went dry as he rubbed himself against me, then smelled my neck letting out a sigh of relief.

"So much better. Thank you."

I laughed. "Your wolf is settling." I could feel the aggression ebbing that had been there only moments earlier.

"A lot, yeah."

"That's crazy."

"Is it? You're my mate, Josie. Of course he's going to freak out having Damon's scent on you even if we know he was no threat to us."

I stared at him and for a moment I forgot to breathe. I was in no way prepared for him to just say the words aloud.

Mate. I was his mate.

Mine! my wolf said.

Mine, I agreed.

"Are you okay?" he asked.

"Yeah, I just wasn't expecting you to just blurt it out like that."

He frowned. "Josie, you're my one true mate. Do you deny that?"

He was watching me and there was so much hope in his eyes.

He reminded me of the little boy I once knew who only wanted to please everyone and protect me from imaginary bad guys.

I shook my head.

"Thank God."

He walked over and sat on the bed and patted the spot next to him for me to join him.

Hesitantly, I did.

"You asked why Damon did what he did. Well, when I first arrived here at the ARC I met a girl. I liked her a lot, but we were not compatible in any way. We both knew it, but we dated for a bit anyway and become really great friends."

"Karis?" I guessed.

His face lit up. "Yes, Karis. Well at the same time I was dating Karis, Damon's wolf caught her scent."

"Which was on you?"

"Oh yeah. Man did he hate me. No one could understand why and later we realized it was because I carried her scent."

"So that was truly just payback?"

"Yup."

"But he didn't really seem to like you, but you're still friends with her?"

He laughed and the sound warmed me all over.

"It's complicated. He's not thrilled about it, or at least he acts that way. In truth he's out of town a lot these days. Someday he will be Alpha of the Alaskan Pack and Karis will be their Pack Mother. When he's in training up north, he worries about his mate. The others think I've been pining for her since freshman year, and I get a lot of shit about it. In truth, Damon and I egg it on. It's almost like a sick game between us."

"But you don't hate each other?"

"How could I hate someone who makes my best friend so happy?"

"But he doesn't really hate you, either. I mean when you growled at him, he really changed his attitude quickly."

"Because he knew there was only one reason I would ever do that no matter how much crap he gave me."

I sucked in a breath and forced myself to say it. "Only for a true mate."

"Yup. So, to clear the air, despite what you might hear,

Damon and I are cool. It is true that when he's out of town I spend a lot of time with Karis. Usually, yes. That is until she kicks me out. What the guys around here don't know is that Damon asks me to keep an eye on her while he's gone."

"Why would he do that?"

He grinned. "Because when I found out that Karis had found her true mate, I backed away gracefully. There is no way I would come between that, and he knows it. I'm not saying we're besties or anything, but we have an understanding."

"Why are you telling me all of this?"

"Because I saw the look of hurt in your eyes when Brian was teasing me at the movie. I don't ever want to hurt you, Josie. And I'll only ever be completely honest with you."

"Thank you for saying that."

"You need to know that Karis is one of the most important people in my life."

Hearing him say that about another woman hurt. I couldn't help it.

He reached for my hands and took them in his.

"Look at me, Josie."

I looked up into his dark blue eyes almost the same color as mine.

"I'd like you to meet her, and I really hope you two can be friends. But I will never choose her over you. If my relationship with her makes you uncomfortable, you just need to let me know."

"Tyler, I can't ask you to stop being friends with someone just because she's a female."

"Yes, you can. You can ask me absolutely anything."

I felt like things were getting serious too quickly.

I grinned. "Okay, what are you majoring in?"

He laughed. "Easy one, accounting and finance."

I crinkled up my nose. "Why?"

"I like math and I'm good at it, but that was two questions and I think you should answer them as well."

"Fair enough, nursing, and because I enjoy helping people."

"What's your favorite color?" I asked him.

"Dark blue like the ocean waters," he responded without hesitations.

My mouth gaped open. That's what he would say when we

were kids.

He brushed my hair back behind my ears and gave me a quizzical look like he was trying to piece together a puzzle.

"Like the color of your eyes."

I smiled and nodded.

"I had forgotten about that."

"So it's not your favorite color?"

"It is. I just forgot why until now."

Everything about my schoolgirl crush on this boy was bubbling to the surface.

"Don't you want to know mine?" I teased.

"Purple," he said, "unless that's changed."

"It hasn't."

He looked pretty proud of himself for remembering that.

"So, who did you take to prom?" he asked.

"Pass."

"What? That's an easy one."

"Nope. Next question."

He groaned. "Fine, who was your first kiss?"

I snorted. "Easy. That would be you."

He laughed. "What? We were like five. Does that even count?"

I shrugged. "It counted to me."

His chest puffed up a little and his grin turned wicked.

"I can do a lot better than that now, you know."

I had a feisty comeback right on the tip of my tongue, something about him pointing out that he had plenty of experience in this department, but he closed the gap between us and captured my mouth with his.

I froze.

How could I explain to him that he had been my only kiss?

I had no idea what I was doing, but as his lips moved against mine, I lost myself in the sensations he created, and I kissed him back.

When he moaned, I smiled against his lips and became a little more daring.

His tongue coaxed my lips apart and dipped into my mouth.

The thought of that had always made me want to gag, but it was nothing like I was prepared for. My own tongue seemed to know exactly what to do as it twirled with his, exploring, learning, craving even more.

Soft needy sounds escaped me, and he deepened the kiss. I was like putty in his hands. My head was swimming in desire. I'd never imagined a kiss could feel so good.

I wanted more. I needed something, but I didn't know what exactly. Tyler did though and that thought sobered me quickly.

It was kind of pathetic to admit I'd been pining for him my entire life. Even though I'd come to terms with the fact that I just used that as a shield to avoid getting close to people. Everyone I'd ever let close to me had hurt me, except Tyler.

I should be rejoicing in the fact that he was here, and he was finally mine, but instead, I could feel myself pulling away, ready to sabotage it all.

I had waited for him, but he hadn't waited for me. That irrational thought stung.

I slowed the kiss and pulled away from him. My lips were swollen and no doubt my checks were a rosy red.

"I should probably go," I said in a husky voice I didn't even recognize.

He shook his head. "No."

"You can't keep bossing me around, Tyler."

"I know. I'm sorry. I just don't want you to go. We were just catching up."

I shot him a look.

He laughed.

"Before that. I mean we were genuinely catching up. Don't go. Please?"

I could feel my resolve cracking. Even as a kid I had never been able to tell him no. He had led me headfirst into more trouble and danger than I'd ever experienced before or after. It had been thrilling.

As my heart started to race, I realized it was still thrilling. Just being near him excited me.

He held up his hands. "I promise to be on my best behavior. No more kisses unless you ask for them."

My cheeks heated. I wasn't sure I was brave enough to do that.

"Boy Scout's honor," he said making peace signs with his

fingers.

I snorted. "You were never a Boy Scout."

"Hey, you don't know. A lot happened between age six and now."

I grabbed his hand and lifted a third finger and mashed them together.

"A real Boy Scout would know that."

"You were a Boy Scout?"

I laughed and shook my head. "No. But Amber's little brother was, and I used to babysit him a lot, including taking him to Scouts."

He groaned and shook his head. "Fine, I'm busted. But will you still stay?"

I bit my lip and nodded.

He dove back into asking me questions again probably sensing that was mostly safe territory.

It didn't take long before I was starting to yawn. I looked at my watch and couldn't believe it was nearly one in the morning.

"Amber's going to freak out."

"Brian's staying over there tonight. She knows you're here with me."

I groaned. "Then she's really going to be freaking out."

"What does that mean?"

"I'm not the kind of girl who has sleep overs with boys, Tyler."

He growled at the thought, then grinned and tackled me down on the bed as I squealed. I had no idea what he was doing, but somehow, he managed to get me down on the bed laid out with him behind me.

He wrapped his arms around me, essentially pinning me into place.

I was overwhelmed by his scent and heat surrounding me. I also had never felt safer or more cherished.

"Stay, for old time's sake. We used to have the best sleepovers."

I giggled. "I don't remember you spooning me like this."

He kissed my shoulder and this time I didn't jump, already on overload with his body wrapped around mine.

"Even then I always wanted to just hold you and keep you

safe."

I had no words to respond, but I didn't move as my body relaxed and I drifted off to sleep enveloped in Tyler.

Tyler

Chapter 7

Waking up with Josie in my arms was everything. I knew I would be perfectly content starting my day that way every morning for the rest of my life.

It was weird. I always knew I wouldn't fight a true mate bond, yet I was still surprised at how simple everything felt with Josie.

Sure, I'd wanted to rip Damon's throat out for putting his scent on her, but that was only a fleeting thought. I was far more concerned with getting that smell off of her than anything. Now that she was covered in my scent, my wolf and I were perfectly content and far more at peace than I'd felt in a long time.

There was a light knock on my door.

I double checked to make sure Josie was covered even knowing she was fully dressed in my clothes.

"Yeah?" I asked.

Pete peeked his head into the room and then grinned down at me.

"Hey, I just wanted to make sure you were okay. The guys said you were either drunk, high, or mating the way you were acting last night." He chuckled.

I groaned. "I should have known."

His eyes widened and I knew it was because I hadn't denied the mating part.

"Is this Amber's friend?"

"Josie," I told him. "Shh, she's still sleeping."

"No, I'm not," she said in a sleepy voice.

I glared at Pete.

"Sorry," he whispered.

I pulled her closer to me. When she stiffened in my arms and looked up at me with big eyes I just grinned.

I couldn't even be embarrassed by the fact I was turned on this morning and unable to hide the evidence of that from her. Even with Pete in the room I didn't think it was going to go away without help.

"Jo-jo, this is Pete, my other roommate," I said.

She looked up at me without even acknowledging Pete.

"There are some things you don't need to remember," she groaned.

I laughed enjoying her minor distress over the old nickname she'd used.

"Alright, Tan…"

I covered her mouth with my hand.

"Okay, no childhood nicknames, ever. Truce?"

She nodded.

When I let go, she turned towards Pete. "Hi Pete."

"Hi." He gawked at us for a minute and then huffed. "True mates?"

I nodded.

"Okay. It was bound to happen to one of us, right? I'm glad it was you and not Brian."

"Why's that?" Josie asked.

I was grateful she didn't seem upset that I'd just admitted everything to Pete. She hadn't even flinched. That had to be improvement, right?

"We all like Amber and would hate to see her hurt like that. Tyler swore off girlfriends freshman year."

"Karis?" Josie asked him.

"Not surprised he's already told you about her, but no. There was a string of them after her. Never anyone serious though. Plus, even if he's going to hook up with someone, he would never bring her back here until it was serious, and there's only one way I know of that Tyler would be serious about a girl."

Josie froze and I glared at Pete.

"Really?"

"Oh, sorry. That's not what I meant, it's just you, you must be important to him to be here."

"I get it, Pete," she said, but I could feel her wolf was unsettled by his blabbering.

He sighed. "Sorry. I'm studying all day and need to go. It was nice meeting you, Josie. If you need help moving stuff over later, just let me know."

I frowned. I really hadn't considered that. "We'll see," I said noncommittedly.

"Pete seems nice," she said after he left.

"He's a great guy. He hasn't been around much this semester though. I wish I knew what was up with him."

She rolled to her stomach and turned to look at me. "I should probably get back to Amber's."

"Or not," I said brushing her hair out of her face.

"Do you plan to just keep me locked up in here for the rest of my life?"

I shrugged. "That could be arranged."

Her face turned serious. "Actually, it can't. I fly home in two days, Tyler. I'm not from here, remember?"

A low growl erupted from me.

Two days?

There was no way I was going to be okay with her walking out of my life again in just two days. I would never be okay with that.

"Why?" I asked.

"What?"

"Why do you have to fly back in two days?"

"Because I already bought the ticket and I start my new job next week."

"Then give me a week at least."

"Tyler, I can't just uproot my life like that."

"Yes, you can. I'll take care of you."

She stared at me with those big blue eyes that were slicing through my heart.

"You can't ask me to do that," she whispered.

"Well, I'm asking."

She sat up looking devastated and I had no idea why.

She shook her head and before I could even say another word, she jumped up and ran from the room.

"What the hell?"

I ran after her, but she was fast.

"Woah, what's going on?" Tim asked as I reached the common room.

"Redhead, where'd she go?"

Hudson pointed to the door.

I walked out on the porch and looked around, but Josie was nowhere to be seen.

"Where the hell did she go?" I yelled.

My body was starting to shake all over, and I could feel fur spouting from my hands.

"Shit! This again?" Hudson asked. "I'm not sure if this place is blessed or cursed."

"That was your mate?" Holden asked.

"Please, like we don't know those signs by now. This house is ridiculous," Hudson continued.

"We'll help you find her," Tim said.

"She's not from here and I don't know if she knows how to get back to Amber's on her own."

"Okay, just stay calm and don't freak out."

Tim leaned in and sniffed me.

"What the hell are you doing?"

"Getting her scent."

"You can't let your wolf out, that's my mate."

Tim's wolf was strong, like Alpha level strong and he had a lot of trouble controlling it. I knew he was doing a lot better lately, but I wasn't willing to risk testing that theory on Josie. There was no way in hell I was going to let him near her while in his fur.

"It's okay. I'm getting stronger. I can do this. My wolf's a great tracker."

"Screw that, I'll handle it myself," I said leaving them sitting there as I ran from the house.

I shifted and caught on to her scent. My wolf howled.

Suddenly three more wolves were by my side, including Tim's.

I growled.

Tim's wolf barked at me, and I knew there was no point in arguing. I wasn't going to settle until I knew Josie was safe.

I wasn't stomaching the idea of her leaving in two days, but that didn't explain why she'd gotten so upset and ran away like that.

I pushed my wolf to go faster as her scent grew stronger. She had just reached the steps to Amber's dorm when I saw her.

I howled as the others came to an abrupt halt behind me.

I stood there, my wolf wailing as I watched her.

She turned and saw me. There were tears in her eyes

"I'm sorry," she whispered and ran up the stairs.

I was frozen in place, shocked.

Hudson's wolf tried to nudge me back towards the house, but I couldn't move.

The pain of rejection was paralyzing.

I wasn't sure how long I stood there, but eventually I walked closer to the stairs and laid down. I would wait there forever if I had to.

I could have shifted and walked inside, but I didn't have any clothes with me, and somehow, I knew Josie wouldn't be happy to talk about it while I was naked. Plus, I didn't know what to say to her. I wanted to understand, but at that moment I couldn't get past the pain and hurt she caused by running away and then turning her back on me.

The guys protested. They even shifted and begged me to come back to the house. I wouldn't budge, or rather my wolf wouldn't budge. I was in no condition to fight him.

Every time the door opened, my hopes rose as I lifted my head and each time I was disappointed all over again.

Tim's wolf stayed with me as if he were on guard, but the twins left only to return later with even more of our brothers in tow.

"What happened?" Chad asked.

"We don't know exactly. He was in his room with the girl and then she ran out looking upset and Tyler just lost it. He shifted and followed her scent here," Hudson explained.

"Does she know he's here?" Jackson asked.

"Yeah, she stopped and looked back, apologized, and ran inside crying," Holden added.

What had I done? All I did was ask her to stay. Why was that so traumatic? I couldn't understand it.

My wolf whimpered and then sat back and howled in mourning trying to reach our mate.

The silence that returned was heartbreaking.

I wasn't in a position to go inside. I was terrified of pushing her even further away. So I laid there and waited in the cold for her to come to me instead.

"It's supposed to snow tonight," Hudson told the guys. "Do we just leave him out here?"

"Did any of you contact Pete or Brian?"

The twins looked at each other, and then pulled out their phones and started calling even more people.

I just wanted them all to go away and leave me alone.

"Pete's not picking up," Holden said.

"Hey, you need to get over here. We're outside Kenston Hall. Oh, really? Well, hurry and get out here then." Hudson hung up the phone. "Brian's inside. He's on his way."

Even knowing he was coming, the second the door opened, my wolf perked up with hope that it would be Josie. The sense of loss and rejection slammed into me again seeing Brian there instead.

I couldn't believe how much it hurt. How could one girl that I'd just reconnected with after more than fifteen years have this much control over me?

While it terrified me, I'd gladly submit if she'd just come out and talk to me.

My wolf howled that haunting sound again.

"Shit, this is bad," Chad said.

"We're starting to draw an audience," Holden warned.

They all circled up around me keeping me out of view from others. If someone tried to get too close, Tim growled at them, and Tim's wolf was not something anyone wanted to cross.

Brian walked over with a scowl on his face.

"What the hell are you doing, Tyler? Get out of here. It's bad enough you made Josie cry, now you're just making an ass of yourself. Man up already. She said, no."

I thought my heart was going to break in two. I couldn't stand here with all their pity any longer.

My wolf jumped to his feet and took off running for the woods.

My brothers stayed behind, but Tim's wolf followed. When I

reached the edge of the woods I turned around and snapped at him. He backed off, but I knew he was just giving me distance while he continued to stalk me.

The temperature was dropping fast, and large fluffy white flakes began to fall from the sky. I'd always loved the snow, but just then it felt more like occasional icy little knives pricking at my fur but I was so numb I barely even felt it.

I could still feel the bond with Josie, though. I didn't know how to sever that connection, but I'd give just about anything to know if it meant stopping the pain.

My wolf growled at the thought.

Mine! he wailed before howling again.

Josie

Chapter 8

"He's still out there, Brian. The snow's really starting to come down now. Someone needs to go and get him. This is ridiculous," Amber said.

I had run like a coward. All he'd ask was for me to stay. It should have been an innocent enough request. I should have been elated even, but all I had thought of was how time and time again I'd been forced to pack up and leave my life behind to accommodate my parents or my parents' friends. It was always someone else's agenda that I was forced to accept. It shouldn't have to be that way with a mate.

I should have just talked to him, but it freaked me out so badly that I just ran.

The more I thought about it, the more I cried.

Amber kept asking what was wrong, but I couldn't tell her. I didn't even know if I could explain it.

They still didn't know that he was my true mate.

Brian was pissed, thinking Tyler had hurt me or tried to, but he had it all wrong, I was the one hurting him—hurting both of us.

"He made his choice," Brian told her.

"We don't even know what happened, but he's your friend. Listen to him. It's awful."

I could hear him. No matter how much I tried to dampen the noise, his wolf spoke right to my soul, and it was killing me.

I tried to tell myself that I was doing what I had to do. I was a survivor. I'd always been, and I would make it through this too.

I was battling an internal war.

Why was I acting this way? This was Tyler. He was all I'd ever wanted in life.

When his wolf howled again, I wiped my tears and got up and left the room. Amber followed me as I knew she would, so I went into the bathroom.

She sighed and walked back into her room to talk to Brian.

I snuck out while she wasn't looking.

I had to find him. I couldn't take it anymore. His howls were heart wrenching, and it was a double edge sword because I knew I was causing it.

I felt so guilty that I had to go and make it right, or at least better.

He deserved an explanation. He deserved a lot, far more than me.

I could not and would not just uproot my entire life again, not for anyone, not even him. I didn't expect him to understand, but I did feel that at least I owed him that much because I didn't want to live my life as a coward either.

Maybe there was a way to break the bond and then he could continue on with his life and I could go back to my life… my pathetic, friendless, lonely life.

Was that what I really wanted? What I needed?

I couldn't think straight and wasn't capable of making such a decision.

I opened the door and stepped outside. The wind had kicked up and there was already close to an inch of snow on the ground and accumulating quickly.

I was still in his shirt and shorts. Even with my wolf to help warm my body I knew I had no business being out in this weather.

Still, I threw caution to the wind, and I set out in the direction I felt most pulled to. It was almost like I had some sort of special compass, and it was pointing right for Tyler.

I came to the edge of some woods and stopped. I looked around me. It was getting harder to see where I'd just come from.

I almost turned back, but then he howled again.

"Tyler!" I yelled and took off running towards the sound.

I ran for a while and then stopped. I turned in a circle and realized I had no idea what direction I'd just come from. I was already lost, and the snow was falling so heavily that visibility was terrible.

"Tyler!" I yelled again.

Time passed and I kept moving.

My fingers were growing numb, and I knew that if I didn't find shelter soon I would need to shift and hope my wolf could find her way back to Amber's.

Lost and confused, I knew I'd made a huge mistake, more than one if I were being honest.

And then, there he was again calling to me.

"Tyler!" I cried out, even knowing his wolf was too far away to hear me over the wind cutting through the trees.

I tried to run towards him and fell into the snow. There was a small embankment that I rolled down. I sat there in the cold and cried.

I'd ruined everything and felt like I'd truly hit rock bottom. I had never had it easy by any means, but my life wasn't so bad, was it? I did have a few friends, like Amber. I missed her, sure, but she said she was planning to return to Virginia when she graduated in the spring.

I had met a few people at nursing school too. I mostly kept them at arm's length, but I could make a better effort on that.

It wasn't any of them that was the problem, it was me.

I pretended to be an optimist who had her shit together, but I was so far from it.

I wasn't weak though. I'd always been a survivor. I didn't understand why I was acting so ridiculously.

Yes, I did. It was these damn hormones.

I'd always been Tyler Klein obsessed. I should be rejoicing to find out he was my one true mate, but these stupid hormones were making me crazy. I couldn't turn them off. I felt everything. Every lonely night talking to a fake version of this man. Every fear, every concern I'd ever had that I'd shared with Tyler in my own way, and yet he didn't know even the basic things about me, like the fact that I needed roots and stability. I wasn't the girl who just packed up and moved across the country on a whim, not even for him.

A large wolf walked into view. I had only glimpsed Tyler's

wolf for a moment before I'd run inside to hide like a coward. I knew this wasn't him.

I scooted backwards until I was teetering on the edge of a cliff. I glanced over my shoulder realizing that if I moved any further I was going to fall thirty feet or more into the icy cold lake.

I froze, my heart thumping hard in my chest.

The wolf didn't growl or approach me. He stared at me for a minute and then shifted into human form.

"Josie, don't move," he said. "Tyler, get over here," he yelled as he slowly descended the hill I'd fallen down.

Tyler's wolf approached and peered down at me. The guy was already halfway down the hill and I was too cold and scared to move.

Seeing Tyler helped to calm me a bit.

Then the wolf growled, and my heart nearly leapt from my throat.

I turned wild eyes towards the man, suddenly seeing him as a threat.

"Knock it off," the guy told Tyler's wolf. "You're scaring her, can't you see that?"

The wolf whimpered and shifted. Tyler stood there looking down and assessing the situation.

"Tim, watch out," he warned just as the guy lost his footing and came sliding down going much too fast. "Josie, grab him!"

I didn't hesitate as I reached out and took his hand as he sailed right past me. I held on for dear life.

Tim was heavier than I expected for such a lanky guy as he dangled over the edge trying desperately to find his footing.

"Don't let go," I said feeling far more confident than I felt. "Do you hear me?"

Tim's eyes locked on with mine and he gave a slight nod.

"Tyler, you have to go for help," I yelled. "Hurry!"

"I can't leave you," he said as he started to make his way down the hill.

"No!" I cried. "If you slip, I don't think I can hold you both. We need ropes or something."

"I can't leave you, Josie," he said again.

"You have to. Go!"

He looked so torn and I hated putting him in that position. In the end, he made the right choice and took off out of view. I said a quick prayer that he would get back in time. I wasn't sure how much longer I could hold on. It felt as though my shoulder was being ripped from its socket.

"Hold on, Tim. He's gone for help."

Tim was silent. I dared a look down and fought back a wave of dizziness really seeing the dilemma we were in.

"If I can swing over just a few more inches, I think I can get a good enough footing to climb back up. Do you think you can hold me?" he asked calmly.

"I don't know," I told him honestly. "Which way?"

"My right, closer to you."

My back was against a tree that I prayed would continue to hold. I couldn't exactly turn or improve my situation much.

"Count it down and I'll lean. I don't know it if will be enough, but that's the best I've got at this angle."

"Okay. On three. One. Two. Three."

I leaned as far away from him as I could pulling him with me as he swung closer.

I grabbed hold of a branch and used every ounce of strength I had to hold on. There was a loud pop and I screamed in pain. I couldn't even feel my hand after a moment.

"Did it work?" I yelled.

The pressure on my hand lifted as Tim scrambled up to safety and collapsed in front of me.

"Yeah. It worked. Is your arm okay?"

"Dislocated I think."

"I'm so sorry. I felt it go and thought I was a goner."

I laughed. "I can't really feel it."

"Let's hope that's cold and adrenaline."

He reached down and ripped off the bottom of Tyler's shorts I was still wearing. He took a piece from each leg that he tied together to make it long enough to fashion a sling and secure my injured arm.

"Thanks," I said sniffling from the pain and trying not to cry for fear my tears would just freeze to my cheeks.

It was so cold.

"You were really lucky to land on that tree," he told me.

"Don't remind me. Watching you slide off the edge like that

was bad enough. Makes me want to throw up just thinking about what could have happened."

He chuckled. "I'm Tim by the way. One of Tyler's fraternity brothers."

"Josie," I said.

"Kind of put that much together. Were you looking for him?"

I nodded. "It was stupid, I know. I just couldn't stand hearing him howl like that any longer. It feels like I've been out here for hours."

"I'd tell you to shift and let your wolf warm you back up, but with that arm, it's not safe for you to shift."

"I'd be too worried she'd freak out and slide off the edge anyway. I'm better off in my skin until we get out of here."

"You're probably right."

"What were you doing here?"

Tim shrugged. "My wolf has listening issues. We're working on it. He's very protective over those I care about."

I relaxed and smiled. "Tyler."

"He's president of the DOGs and my fraternity brother. So yeah. I couldn't have convinced my wolf to leave him like that. We could be here a while. Do you want to talk about what happened?"

I sighed. "You wouldn't understand."

"Try me."

There was something about Tim. He seemed a little dorky, but there was something soothing about him too. It made me feel like I really could talk to him, or it was possible that was just the hypothermia setting in.

I shivered.

"Tyler's my one true mate," I blurted out.

He laughed. "That much is kind of obvious. I've known Tyler for a while now and he would never act so out of character for anything else."

"It's just crazy. This mating stuff will literally drive you insane."

"I remember," he said.

My head shot up to look at him again. He smiled and turned his head so I could see the bond mark on his neck.

"You're mated?"

"Yeah, over a year now."

"But you look so young," I blurted out. He didn't even look twenty yet.

He chuckled and shrugged. "We don't get to control when or where we find the one. I guess that just makes me lucky."

"Lucky? To be tied down so early in life?"

"Yeah, are you kidding? Jess is the best. All that scary adulting stuff out there, I don't have to face that alone. I am crazy in love with my mate and wouldn't have it any other way."

I didn't know how to process that. He wasn't just mated, but in love with his mate. The two didn't necessarily go hand in hand, though I already knew in my heart I would always love Tyler. But to have him love me back? That terrified me because it seemed so much bigger than just a mated bond.

"I'm assuming things aren't going so well right now, and you're right the mating call can drive a person insane, but it's all worth it, Josie. All of it."

"He wants me to stay," I blurted out.

"Is that really so bad?"

"Yes. What if you had finally found a home and stable environment to live and then you just happen to cross paths with your mate and she asks to leave it all behind and move across the country just to be with her?"

Tim gave me a weird look and then burst out laughing.

"It's not funny."

"No it isn't. I'm sorry. It's just that, you pretty much did just describe my life."

"What?"

"I didn't grow up under very good circumstances, Josie. My mom left when I was young. I have no memory of her. My father was an abusive alcoholic. I was raised in a rundown trailer park on the wrong side of the tracks. My brother Ollie pretty much raised me and my brothers. And then he found his true mate. Peyton's the best. She's a Collier wolf and she bought us a big house that we restored. She bought me a bed. I had never slept in one before. She fiercely loved my brother, his daughter, my other brothers, and me. I went to college an hour away from there. She insisted I live on campus, but I would have been perfectly content at home with my family. But then I met Jessie. She was already going to school here and I knew she would be returning. I had a choice to make. Stay in Wyoming, or leave everything I cared about and follow her here."

"You chose to come here," I whispered.

"It was never really a choice."

"There's always a choice," I argued.

He nodded. "True. The choice between who I was comfortable being, and who I was meant to be. I was born to be Jessie's mate. There is nothing more important than that to me. I would follow that girl to the ends of the world and back knowing that as long as we're together, everything's going to be okay."

I considered that. "But you gave up everything for her."

"See, that's where you're wrong. My family, my home, and a huge piece of my heart is still in Wyoming, but I talk to them almost daily. We go home for visits. Life comes with compromises, Josie. But I promise you it's worth it."

"I'm scared," I admitted to him.

"Have you talked to Tyler about this?"

I shook my head.

"You really need to."

"But he wants me to stay."

"He's a mating male. Of course he wants you to stay. Just having you out of his sight right now I guarantee has his wolf going psychotic. He needs to be near you right now more than ever. And you need him too."

I pulled my knees up to my chest and tried not to jostle my arm too much.

"How did you know that leaving and following her here was the right choice?"

"That was simple. I had more to lose staying than leaving."

"But..."

"No but, Josie. Staying would have lost me my mate. But leaving didn't lose me my family. Besides, when it comes down to it, I need her more than I need them. And truth be told, if me staying had been best for us, then we would have made that choice together. Is that it? You're scared to leave your family? Talk to him. You might be surprised just how much he's willing to leave behind for you."

I sighed. I didn't really have any family to leave, though, only the safe haven I had cultivated for the last few years and held onto for dear life.

Tyler

Chapter 9

My wolf and I were at odds like never before. The rational human part of me knew that leaving Josie and Tim to go get help was the right thing to do. My animalistic nature strongly disagreed, and my wolf was vocalizing his displeasure in my head over, and over again.

I was naked running through the woods. I didn't trust my wolf in this state to obey and do what needed to be done, so I was stuck in my skin in the middle of a snow storm.

It was freezing out and Josie was only in my shirt and gym shorts. If I didn't hurry, she could freeze.

Fortunately, I knew these woods like the back of my hand.

In record time I was running up the stairs of the doghouse.

"Woah! Naked man," Holden complained shielding his mate from looking at me.

"He's back, ladies and gentlemen," Hudson announced. "Wait, what's wrong?"

"Grab some rope and extra blankets quickly. We have to hurry."

I didn't take time to explain. I did run to my room and grab two of my coats putting one on and carrying the other. I also grabbed the blankets from my bed and two ropes I used to belay when rock climbing.

When I came back to through, no one had moved.

"What is wrong with you people, hurry! If Josie let's go, Tim could die."

I wasn't being dramatic either. He'd been dangling over the edge of the cliff when I took off and I didn't know how long Josie could hold on. I didn't want her to live with that on her conscious. Time was of the essence.

Everyone scrambled to listen this time and soon I was running back to the woods as fast as I could. I hadn't needed my wolf to show me the way, I knew exactly where my mate was.

"Josie!" I yelled as I got closer.

"Down here," she yelled again. The hysteria I was expecting was missing from her voice, but that only freaked me out more.

As I approached, I slid on my stomach across the snow. It stung like a sonofabitch, but I knew it was the safest way to approach without risking falling the way Tim had.

"Stay down, it's slippery," I warned the others. "And tie off the rope to that tree, quickly."

I was already suiting up to repel down. If it weren't for the snow I wouldn't need it, but given what had happened, I wasn't chancing it.

I finally peeked down, and Josie was still sitting next to the tree. Her arm was in a sling and Tim was sitting naked next to her.

A growl rumbled through my chest.

Was she injured?

What had happened?

It also registered that Tim was naked next to her, and he was holding her rubbing her arms. Logically I knew it was for warmth, but that didn't stop my wolf from seeing red.

"Shit! Tim, get away from her. He's coming down and his wolf is nearly feral at this point. He's barely holding on here."

I took a deep breath trying to calm myself. When I had the go-ahead, I slowly began lowering myself towards them. It didn't take long. It was only about a ten foot drop.

"Feed me a little more line," I said after falling just shy of being able to touch her.

"Josie? Are you okay?"

"You're going to have to touch him. His wolf is on edge and I'd like to make it out of here alive. Regardless, he'll never hurt you," Tim explained to her in a calm voice.

I fell to my knees at her feet, she leaned forward and threw her arm around me.

"I'm sorry," she sobbed. "I'm so sorry."

Instantly, my wolf calmed. It was a little unnerving really.

"It's okay. I'm here now. Shh. It's okay."

I squeezed her close to me and she whimpered in pain.

I pulled back my wolf thrusting forward and trying to regain control.

"She's fine, Tyler. Tell him, you're going to be fine, Josie," Tim coached her.

"I'm fine. I just want to get out of here. Please."

I nodded as her words cut through the haze around my vision.

"Send me down the other rope so Tim can come back up."

Someone up top listened. I tested the rope for safety and then passed it to Tim.

"It'll hold. Just take it slow and watch your footing as much as possible.

"I got it," he said. "And thanks, Tyler. Your girl is something else. Saved my life. I owe her big time."

Josie's cheeks turned impossibly darker. "It was nothing," she insisted.

"Don't sell yourself short. You kept a solid head out here and you were able to pull me up to safety."

My heart soared in pride.

Tim slowly started making his way up.

I tried to ignore the fact that she was injured and focused on having her in my arms. We took our time as we started our ascent.

"One step at a time. I'm right behind you and I'm not letting you go."

"Okay," she said softly.

I praised her every step of the way.

A cheer went up as Tim reached the top. We weren't that far behind him.

I kept Josie close to me, her injured arm tucked against my side so as not to jostle it too much. I had given Tim my spare coat and wrapped two blankets around Josie to try and warm her up.

I tried not to think about how she was hurt because of me. I'd done this to her. If I hadn't gotten butt hurt and run off into the woods, she wouldn't have come looking for me. If she wasn't in the woods to begin with, she never would have gotten hurt.

"Don't do that to yourself," Tim warned me.

"What?" I snapped.

"What happened wasn't your fault. Just be thankful you were there to get us help." He clapped me on the shoulder. "Trust me, the what ifs will eat you alive."

He sounded like he was talking from experience. His words subdued my wolf some.

The brothers kept watching me closely. I knew they were worried about me. They had every right to be worried. I hated it, but if the roles were reversed and it was any of them in my shoes, I'd be worried too.

"Come on. Let's get you inside."

Josie didn't resist as I led her through the woods and back towards main campus. When we reached the edge of the woods the guys veered off to the left towards the doghouse but I stopped. I couldn't force her to come back to me. I needed it to be her choice.

"Do you want to go back to Amber's?" I asked her.

She looked up at me and shook her head. "She's going to be worried though."

"We can call her once you've warmed up and we get your arm fixed."

"It's my shoulder actually. It's dislocated."

"What?" I growled.

She cringed. "I didn't shift. There's no permanent damage done."

Instead of taking her back to my room or to Amber's dorm, I instead walked her straight to the clinic.

For the most part there wasn't much of a need for a twenty-four hour clinic at a shifter college. We rarely got sick and most injuries were healed on their own, but you just never knew, and times like this was exactly why they kept it around.

"What can I do for you?" the nurse asked when we walked in.

"She's dislocated her shoulder," I explained.

"Oh dear. Take a seat. We'll get you fixed up in a jiffy."

True to her word, she came around right away and checked Josie's shoulder for herself.

"I don't even want to know how this happened. Sweetie, take

her good hand so she has something to bare down on. This is going to hurt, but only for a second."

I growled at her and she just laughed.

"You think I haven't dealt with my fair share of mating males around here? Just let her squeeze your hand. This will be over quickly."

Josie's big blue eyes stared up at me.

"You're doing great Josie."

I heard the crunch and saw the tears spring to her eyes.

The nurse felt around and had her rotate her arm.

"There you go. All better. Take some aspirin if needed. It could be sore for a few hours. Your animal should start to heal any ligament damage soon."

"Huh. That's it?" Josie asked.

"That's it. You'll be good as new in no time."

I thanked the nurse and took Josie's hand in mine as we walked back to the house. I needed that direct connection to her. I had to touch her.

If she had asked to go back to Amber's, I would have taken her, but I would have struggled to leave her there and probably would have slept in the hallway outside of Amber's room if they had kicked me out.

It was embarrassing just how badly I needed her.

Mate! my wolf reminded me.

I didn't just need her, I needed to touch her constantly. It was making me feel a bit like an overprotective ass and I suddenly understood why Damon had acted so insane when mating Karis. Not only was he dealing with all of this, but he also had sudden Alpha powers coming in.

If that happened to me, I'm not sure I wouldn't have killed someone already. I was struggling to keep the aggression at bay as it was, and I was no Alpha.

We didn't talk as we walked across campus.

The guys were all waiting for us when we got back, and Brian and Amber were there too.

Amber ran over and hugged Josie pulling her out of my arms.

I growled and she just glared at me.

Tim stepped in and broke the two apart and then pushed Josie back towards me. I caught her with ease and my wolf instantly settled again.

"Sorry, but we don't need any bloodshed tonight."

Josie turned her blue eyes up towards me. They were filled with concern.

"I'm fine," I tried to reassure her.

"No, he's not," Tim insisted. "But he will be once his wolf is confident she's okay."

"Why didn't you just tell us?" Brian asked. "I wouldn't have yelled at you if I had known she was your mate."

Josie stiffened and I saw her look towards Amber.

"You could have told me," Amber said to her.

"I wasn't ready to talk about it," Josie said.

"Well, I'm here when you are."

"Thanks," she said softly.

Jess walked over and hugged Josie but was careful not to steal her away from me.

"Uh, hi," my mate squeaked.

"Hi. I'm Jessie, Tim's mate. I heard what you did out there. I can't thank you enough. Is your arm okay?"

"It was just dislocated. No permanent damage."

"We stopped by the clinic, and they reset it for her," I explained. "She just needs some rest now."

I was trying to politely excuse us, but that only kicked off more questions as Tim told the story of how Josie had saved his life.

She blushed and I could feel her discomfort in a new way that freaked me out just a little. It seemed too soon for me to be that in tune with her emotions.

All the brothers felt a bit indebted to my girl and suddenly it was like she had a houseful of other protective brothers all wanting to make sure she was okay and offering to get her anything she could possibly want.

They were doting on my mate.

She'd risked her own life and taken injury to save one of us. She had no idea what that meant in this doghouse.

Kian had disappeared for a bit but returned with a steaming cup of hot chocolate. For some reason his hot chocolate tasted better than any other possibly could. He refused to tell anyone his secret, but it was amazing.

He offered a cup to Josie, but she declined.

"Oh no. Take this and drink. You will not be sorry. Kian's hot chocolate is legendary around this place, and he refuses to make it most of the time."

"Well in that case, thanks, Kian."

"For you, anytime. The rest of these assholes have to beg first." He winked at her, but I was too overwhelmed by the support and respect they were all showing her to even growl.

She took a sip of the hot chocolatey goodness and moaned. The sounds shot straight to my groin, and I knew it was time to go.

"Holy crap, Kian. This is amazing!"

The others laughed and nodded in agreement. We all knew it was true, but then Josie licked her lips and I knew we had to leave before I did something stupid to embarrass us both.

"I really appreciate everything, but it's been a long day and the nurse said she needs to rest."

I tried to nudge Josie forward but she wasn't moving.

"You're staying the night again?" Amber asked, pouting.

"Yes, she is," I answered for her.

Josie shot me a look of warning.

"Babe, let her go. His wolf hasn't fully settled yet," Brian said. "But we're talking about this tomorrow," he warned me.

I nodded.

Just then Pete walked in.

"Hey guys. I have a couple dozen messages and you're all here. What did I miss?"

I groaned fearing we'd be here another hour or more explaining things.

"Ask them," I finally said. "We're going to bed."

When I took a step towards the hallway, Josie didn't move. It was like she was frozen to the floor and her cheeks were bright red again.

I carefully took the hot mug from her and then with my free arm I hoisted her over my shoulder and gave a nod goodnight.

I made it halfway down the hallway before her shock wore off.

She smacked my ass and yelled. "This has got to stop. You can't keep going all caveman on me like this."

I chuckled along with the chorus of laughter behind us.

Josie

Chapter 10

Tyler set me down and I crossed my arms and glared at him.

"Again? Really?"

"What? I was just trying to speed things up. Pete just got back, and we'd have been there another hour or more."

He didn't hand me back my mug of hot chocolate, instead he set it down on the desk and then pulled me into his arms. I barely had time to catch my breath when he kissed me.

This time, I knew exactly what to do.

When I lifted my arm up to wrap around his neck, pain shot through it and I winced.

Tyler immediately pulled back. I could feel that his wolf was still on edge.

"I'm okay," I tried to tell him, but he wasn't hearing me.

"Shit! I'll be right back."

He left the room, and my head was literally spinning. I couldn't help but wonder if all kisses were so potent or if it was just his. I was quite certain I never wanted a firsthand answer to that. Tyler had always been it for me. Even if things didn't work out for us, I doubted that would ever change.

I took my cup and sipped the chocolatey goodness.

I was still cold from being outside, but the hot chocolate was helping to warm me, just not as much as being close to Tyler had.

I wondered where he had taken off to? I wasn't going to

venture out to look for him. I'd had enough embarrassment for one day.

He wasn't gone long. When he returned he had a laundry basket full of stuff. He dropped it on the floor and then shrugged out of the coat he had been wearing when he returned to rescue me.

My jaw dropped. "You were naked under that the whole time?"

He chuckled and shrugged. "Didn't want to waste time putting on clothes, just didn't want to freeze to death out there either."

I had never really seen a naked man before. I mean, I had, I just averted my eyes and refused to look. I couldn't stop staring at him now, and I had a feeling that as long as I was looking, he wasn't going to cover himself.

"Josie," he said with a teasing tone to his voice. "Eyes up here, sweetheart."

My cheeks flushed as my head jerked up.

He grinned proudly.

"Sorry," I muttered, forcing myself not to look down again.

"Don't be. You're welcome to look all you want. I'm all yours."

My body tingled all over at his words.

I gulped. "We should talk."

He frowned and nodded. "About why you ran off?"

I had walked right into that one. "Maybe," I said noncommittedly.

"Then what did you want to talk about?"

"I don't know."

"Do you want to tell me why you took off the way you did earlier?"

I shook my head. "No, not yet."

He nodded.

"Could you put some clothes on? It's very distracting."

"Or you could just take yours off and then we'll be evenly matched."

I could tell he was only teasing. He was already walking towards the bucket to pull out something to wear.

A part of me wished I had the courage to just strip for him and see what happened, but that wasn't me. The fact that I even considered doing it scared the shit out of me. Largely because it was exactly the sort of thing my mother would do.

I froze in horror at the thought. I had made a promise to myself that I would never be like her.

"Josie? Are you okay?"

My heart was racing and I was struggling to breathe.

"Josie!"

Tyler wrapped his arms around me, the room spun and then everything turned peaceful. My breathing stabilized and I looked up into his blue eyes and I knew everything was going to be okay.

"Jesus, Josie, you scared the shit out of me. Are you okay?"

Tears pricked my eyes as I nodded.

"I was hyperventilating."

"I noticed."

"But you, your touch stopped it."

"Your touch settles me like that too," he confessed.

I knew that. I'd seen it with my own eyes.

He started to walk back to the laundry to get dressed. I grabbed hold of his hand for dear life.

"Please, don't leave me."

I was scared that my panic attack would resume if he let go of me.

"Okay. You're okay. Give me your hand. I'm just going to turn the light off and then we can go to bed. It's been a long day."

I nodded. "Okay."

He held my hand, never breaking the connection between us as he turned off the lights, and then settled us into bed. I didn't even care that he was still naked, I just needed to feel him close to me.

He crawled in behind me just as we had slept the night before, but this time I rolled over to face him. He wrapped his arms more tightly around me as I rested my head on his chest.

I took a deep breath taking in his woodsy scent and letting it calm me further.

It wasn't enough.

My hand roamed up and down his stomach just feeling the ridges of his abs.

He didn't move. He just laid there, letting me explore.

At first I didn't even realize I was doing that. I was just calming myself. It took a few minutes to realize that he wasn't calm at all.

My hand stilled and then flexed.

"Sorry. I'm mostly okay now."

He reached for my hand and rubbed it up and down his chest.

"Don't ever apologize for touching me."

"But it's making you uneasy."

A deep rumble went through him. I could feel it beneath my hand.

"That's not unease you're sensing, sweetheart."

"Oh," I said. "What is it then?"

He froze and reality struck me. His scent was so strong it was drawing me closer to him. He wasn't uneasy, I was turning him on.

I squeaked and buried my face in his chest. "Sorry. I'm an idiot."

He laughed again and kissed the top of my head. "No you're not."

"I guess it's pretty obvious I haven't exactly had much experience in this department," I confessed. I was glad the lights were out because I knew the blush was spreading down my neck and across my chest.

This was so embarrassing.

He growled, not the aggressive kind, but a sexy sound that made my mouth go dry as I gulped hard.

His arm tightened around me.

"Never?" he asked.

I didn't need him to clarify what he was asking, and I couldn't seem to form the word, but I shook my head against his chest.

Another sexy growl rumbled through him.

He tilted my head up to look at him. "No one?"

I bit my lip and shook my head again.

His lips crashed against mine once again, more possessive than before.

"Mine," he growled against them.

I smiled and kissed him back, parting my lips and waiting for his blessed intrusion that I was certain would come.

I felt like I was floating, but I forced myself back down to Earth and pulled away to look at him.

"That doesn't bother you?"

"Hell no."

"Really?"

"To never share you with anyone? Yeah, I'm positive. You'll never know another man. Just me."

"I've never even kissed anyone but you," I blurted out.

He growled and then groaned. "You're killing me."

"I'm sorry. You just should know."

"Is that why you got freaked out and left this morning?"

"What? No."

He was hurt. I could feel it. I'd done that when I ran out on him.

"I don't want to talk about it, but it wasn't you. It was me. And it had nothing to do with this," I tried to assure him.

I took a deep breath, praying I wouldn't freak out on him again. This wasn't like her. I wasn't like her. I needed to prove that to myself.

This was about me and my mate. I knew the bond was making him just as crazy as it made me. Feeling his warm skin in my hands had helped me, and maybe it would help him too.

I knew I was trying to reason with myself so I didn't chicken out as I sat up and pulled his shirt from my body tossing it on the floor.

His breath caught as he looked down at my exposed breasts.

I reached for his hand and placed it over my heart.

"It wasn't this," I told him again.

I had underestimated just how good I was making him feel by touching him. Well, that was if my touch made him feel even a fraction of the fire he was stoking inside of me as I pressed my body against his.

"Josie," he whispered in a hard voice. I instinctively recognized it as desire.

He wanted me. Me. I could hardly believe it.

The bond pulled us together, but I didn't think it truly caused the craving I had for him.

The funny thing was, I wasn't scared anymore. Being this intimately close to him was a powerful feeling that made me stronger and bolder.

"I want to touch you," he said.

"You already are," I pointed out.

"Not like I want to," he warned.

Goosebumps broke out on my skin and a shrill of excitement ran up my spine.

"Touch me," I whispered, barely audible to my own ears.

He didn't wait for another invitation. His arms wrapped around me and pulled me flush against him. We were skin to skin. I could feel my nipples harden as they rubbed against his hair-dotted chest.

His hands roamed over my back as he kissed me once more.

I didn't even fully understand the feelings of need welling up inside of me, but my body knew what it wanted.

Tyler rolled me onto my back as one hand splayed out across my stomach.

I wanted more.

Small sounds I didn't even recognize came from somewhere within me as he kissed me down my neck and across my shoulder. I shuddered when he stopped to nibble on a spot I was certain he wanted to mark. I gasped when he sucked on the skin there feeling his teeth drag across.

I had no idea if I was ready to bond with him. There was so much we still needed to discuss and figure out, but I wasn't going to stop him.

I was slightly disappointed when he moved on and captured my lips once more.

His hand slowly moved upwards until he was cupping my breast.

He pulled back and looked deep into my eyes.

"Josie?" he asked in a strained voice.

I knew what he wanted. I bit my swollen lip and nodded.

He smiled and kissed me again as he continued. His thumb circled around my erect nipple and I moaned.

He smiled against my lips and began a sultry torture that stirred something inside of me.

"Oh." I gasped.

"Do you like that?" he asked.

"Yes. Oh, yes."

He rolled my nipple between his finger and thumb making my breath catch.

He grinned, and then rolled a little more over me. His knee

settled between my legs. I could feel him thick and hard pressing into my hip. I did that to him.

His head dipped and captured my other breast in his hot wet mouth.

I groaned and my hips bucked, feeling the pressure of his leg between mine. It felt good. So good that I did it again until I was rubbing myself against his leg at a steady pace.

My muscles were tightening and inside I felt as though I were burning.

"Tyler," I whimpered. "Tyler."

"I've got you. I know what you need," he said confidently.

His hand dipped between us inside the waist of the shorts. His teeth grazed against my nipple as his fingers touched me.

I was panting, bucking against his hand. It felt so good. So good. I couldn't seem to stop. It was like I was seeking some unknown destination.

"Tyler. Tyler," I couldn't take it anymore.

I needed him to stop, the sensation was so powerful.

"It's too much," I tried to tell him.

His finger dipped inside me and my hips jerks as every muscle in my body tightened, and then I was set free.

I think I screamed, but then, I was floating.

I should have been embarrassed by my behavior, but nothing had ever felt so good.

Tyler

Chapter 11

I certainly hadn't planned on this. Josie had been so responsive to my touch that I'd almost come with her. Seeing the wonder in her eyes as she clearly experienced her first orgasm had left me speechless and feeling like the king of the world.

I doubted I would ever be able to forget the sounds she made or the way she had cried out my name. She didn't know it, but she had somehow branded herself onto my heart.

I had actually never been with a virgin before, not even my first time. I had no idea what I was missing out on, or maybe it was just her that made me feel this way.

I was quiet, just watching her enjoy the after shocks of it all. I couldn't wait to show her more.

Her heavy breathing started to slow, and she finally opened her eyes again and looked up at me. She wasn't the slightest bit embarrassed, which seemed to be a pretty normal state she lived in.

"Are you okay?" I asked her.

"Pretty sure I've never been better. Are you okay?"

I leaned down and kissed her. "Oh yeah."

She reached up and pulled me back down to her, kissing me this time. I noticed she didn't wince lifting her arm, and hoped that meant her injury was healing quickly.

I didn't think I should push her. I knew she was still a little high, but dammit I was struggling to pull away from her. I wanted her so badly.

Tonight wasn't going to be her first time. I needed to take this slowly and do it right to ensure this girl would be mine forever.

The memory of her running out of here and leaving me was still like a fresh wound. I needed to know why she had left. What had I said or done? Clearly it had nothing to do with sex, she'd certainly made her point about that tonight.

"Tyler?" she asked.

"Yeah."

"Are you okay?"

"What?"

"You sort of spaced out a little."

"I'm sorry." I gave her a chaste kiss.

My body was still thrumming as if that had been the best foreplay of my life, but my mind had begun to wander, filled with so many questions.

I snuggled down next to her and tucked her into my side.

She wiggled against me and my body instantly reacted.

I cursed under my breath, trying to will it to calm down, but having her half naked beside me with the memories of her moans still fresh in my ears, meant it had a mind of its own.

"Um, can I ask you a question that's going to sound dumb and naïve?"

"Josie, you can ask me absolutely anything."

She took a deep breath and seemed to be pep talking herself into saying whatever was on her mind.

"Josie?"

"Okay, so I get the whole sex part and all that, but without it, how exactly do you calm that thing down?"

My dick sprang to life wedged between us and I groaned.

"I told you it was a stupid question."

"It's not, I just think he has a mind of his own and you just perked him back up."

She giggled a little nervously.

"Don't worry about me. I'll be fine. I'll deal with it later."

"But how?"

"I can, um, you know, take things into my own hands."

She rolled back a little and propped herself up on one elbow.

"You mean like you took me in your own hands?"

I didn't want to laugh because I knew she was being serious, but it was too cute.

"Yeah, something like that."

"Show me."

"You really want me to sit here and jack off in front of you?"

Her eyes widened and then she licked her damn lips. I was going to need a very cold shower and soon.

"Please."

I shook my head. "I don't think I will ever be able to tell you no."

She smirked but watched as I fisted my hand around myself.

"That's it?"

"More or less."

"Can I try it?"

"You are trying to kill me, aren't you?"

"No, I just want to learn how to make you feel as good as you just made me feel. Is that really so bad?"

How the hell was I supposed to argue that?

"Lick your hand," I blurted out.

She didn't question it, she just did it.

I took her hand in mine and wrapped it around myself. It felt so good, and far more intimate than anything I'd ever experienced in my life.

Slowly I guided her hand up and down.

She was staring and concentrating so hard.

"Just relax," I said not sure if I was talking to her or myself.

She squeezed just a little and moved a tiny bit faster.

"And this feels good to you?"

"Yes," I said in a strained voice.

Her touch was far more potent than I imagined it would be and I knew I wasn't going to last long. I rolled onto my back and submitted full control to her.

"You'll tell me if you don't like something?" she asked.

"Josie, any way you touch me, I'm going to enjoy. I promise."

She looked up at me and smiled, and then she kissed me. She trailed light kisses down my neck swirling her tongue over one spot in particular that had my canines dropping.

I was already beginning to pant.

She continued her tormenting kisses across my chest, licking, sucking, testing me. When I reacted she stopped and tortured that spot a little longer until I was ready to beg her to finish it.

"Faster," I said through gritted teeth.

"Oh, okay."

She picked up the pace, watching and measuring my reaction. I couldn't just lie there still any longer. I was so close.

Somehow she seemed to recognize that too and moved faster and faster and I closed my eyes and accepted the glorious release.

My body shook and when I opened my eyes again, she had a satisfied smirk on her face, looking pleased with herself.

I got up and grabbed a towel to clean myself off and then her.

She stayed oddly quiet for someone who had so boldly just asked me to teach her how to get me off.

"Let me get you a clean pair of shorts," I said, noticing I'd made a little bit of a mess. Who could blame me for that?

"It's okay," she said, then she took the shorts off and threw them onto the floor. "Just come on back to bed."

I gulped, suddenly feeling like I was the one out of my element here.

I had teased her about taking her clothes off, but at that time, I really didn't expect it to happen. Sleeping next to her like that was going to be sheer torture.

*****

I was wrong. Sleeping next to Josie was as easy as breathing.

I stretched and kissed her shoulder hoping the pain from the dislocation was gone. I thought back through everything that had happened. There was a lot we still needed to discuss, like what had triggered her flight mechanism to run away from me in the first place.

The fact that she had come looking for me and then last night not only let me touch her but wanted to learn how to please me too, gave me hope that things were going to work out okay, but I still had an unsettling feeling that something was wrong.

Josie stretched and gave a sexy little moan.

She rolled over and looked up at me with a sleepy smile. She was so beautiful.

"Good morning," she said, a little shyly.

"Good morning," I said kissing her. "You sleepyhead, can stay in as long as you'd like, but unfortunately I have class in an hour."

If she had asked me to stay, I would have in a heartbeat, but she didn't.

"Will you be here when I get back?" I asked. I had to know.

"I don't know. I haven't thought that far ahead."

I knew she was leaving tomorrow and that had my wolf agitated. How was I going to manage with her on the other side of the country?

I wasn't going to ask her to stay again. I'd been thinking through things a lot and something about that conversation had set her off.

"I'm going to go grab some breakfast from the kitchen. Anything in particular you'd like?"

"Um toast?"

"That's it?"

"I don't know what you have here."

"Anything. I can make you bacon and eggs, pancakes, waffles, oatmeal, cereal, anything you want."

"You cook?"

"I do actually."

"Just eggs and toast then. Bacon takes too long."

"There's probably some pre-cooked bacon."

She scrunched up her nose. "Not the same."

I chuckled, gave her another kiss and forced myself to leave the bed. I did toss on a pair of sweatpants, but not before catching her checking me out.

Brian was in the kitchen when I walked in.

"Hey," I said opening the fridge and pulling out some eggs and bacon.

"Hey. You good?"

"Yeah, I'm fine."

I put the bacon on to fry and then turned to face Brian. He was staring at me and I knew he needed to get stuff off his chest.

"Why the hell didn't you just tell me?"

I shrugged. "I don't know. I was just in shock and trying to deal with it all."

"She's really your true mate?"

I nodded. "She really is."

"Dude, Damon knew before me, didn't he?"

I sighed. "Well, I did growl at him over dinner."

"I thought you were just messing with him."

"I wouldn't joke about something like this."

"Wow. I mean, I guess I'm happy for you. It's weird, though right? Like you don't even know her."

"I know enough."

"I just can't even imagine it," he confessed.

"That's only because it hasn't happened to you."

"And it won't," Brian insisted. "Because I've already requested approval to mate Amber."

"Seriously?"

He nodded.

"Dude, that's great. You two are perfect for each other."

"I think so, too. At first I wasn't sure, you know. I see several of the brothers happily mated to their true mates and it's hard not to wonder if I should wait for that, but I love her. I can't imagine loving anyone else more just because of some weird connection thing that I had no choice in. And then I see you going through all this shit now and remember what they went through before the happy parts, and I know it's just not for me. I'm happy just the way things are, and Amber is too."

"I'm really happy for the both of you. Amber's great."

"You should know, she doesn't think Josie will stay. She didn't say why, but she'd bet against you where that girl's concerned. She's leaving tomorrow, Tyler. I just don't want to see you hurt."

A darkness sunk in as his words rang with truth.

He clapped me on the shoulder. "You know I'll always be here for you no matter what happens, and I promise not to be such an ass about it now that I know."

I chuckled without humor but didn't say anything.

The bacon was done frying, I quickly cooked five eggs for the two of us and made some fresh toast. I buttered the bread, fixed two plates, and headed back to my room.

Josie was just stepping out of the shower.

An alert on my phone went off as I set the plates down on my desk and picked up my phone to check it.

"Is everything okay?" she asked.

I nodded. "Classes are canceled today due to the storm. Apparently, it's still coming down pretty hard out there."

"It is?" she plucked a piece of bacon off one of the plates before checking her phone. "My flight's still showing as on time, but everything for today looks to be canceled. It must really be bad out there.".

I sucked in a sharp breath. "Are you really leaving tomorrow?"

Her big blue eyes stared back at me, and I could feel the pain hiding in them.

"Tyler, I have a life on the other side of the country. I never expected any of this."

Hearing that scared me. I couldn't lose her. I'd just found her again. I pulled her into my arms.

"I know you didn't. I never saw it coming either. But I'm right here. We can figure this out, okay?"

She took a deep breath and nodded. "One day at a time?"

"I can do that."

My wolf was growing more agitated by the moment, but I pushed him aside. If this is what Josie needed, then this is what I had to give her. I had no idea how we were going to make this work. I didn't think I could switch to all online classes to finish out the year, but it wouldn't hurt to ask. Three months, that's all we were talking about. Even if we had to be mostly apart for three months, we'd make it work. I was here on scholarship and never touched my monthly Pack stipend, so I had money. I could spend some of it on flights to Virginia. I could withstand most anything for three months if I had to, as long as I knew she was with me on this.

I couldn't push her to make that choice right now.

One day at a time.

That's what she asked for and that's what I would give her.

Josie

Chapter 12

Tyler was being sweet, too sweet. There was no way I was going to be ready to leave him tomorrow, but I didn't think I had the courage to stay either.

Just one day at a time. I could do that.

His classes were canceled for the day. I had hoped to spend a little more time with Amber while he was busy, but I sensed that I needed this time with him more.

Last night something had shifted. I'd been bold and it had felt incredible.

Being intimate with Tyler was better than anything I could have imagined. But I could feel our bond strengthening. The more time I spent with him, the harder it was going to be to walk away. Still, I couldn't deny him that. I couldn't deny myself that, either.

"If your classes are canceled, what do you want to do today?"

He gave me a wicked grin. "Oh, I can think of a few things. Starting with…" his arms went around me again, but this time he reached behind me and picked up one of the plates and presented it to me. "Breakfast."

I grinned. "Cute."

I took it from him and practically inhaled it. We'd skipped dinner the night before and I had barely touched the lunch Amber had offered me. I was famished.

"There's more here if you need it," Tyler said offering me his plate.

"No. Eat. I just realized I didn't really eat yesterday."

"I can make more."

"I'm good. This was delicious. Thank you."

I didn't like that things felt tense with us today. For once I didn't want to stress about the future or even think about preparing to go home tomorrow. For today I promised myself I'd just live and let my guard down for once.

One day isn't going to change your life forever. You aren't like them.

"Hey, what's wrong?" Tyler asked.

"Nothing," I said giving him a smile.

"Josie, you should probably know that you can't lie to me. I can literally feel when something's off with you. It's the bond, and it's getting stronger."

"We just met, Tyler. It can't be growing yet."

I knew that was a lie because I could feel him too. The truth just terrified me and threatened to destroy my carefully erected, perfectly simple, no surprises life back home.

He took my hands and looked into my eyes. It was kind of weird and he did it a lot. For wolf shifters that was a sign of challenge, but with him it was different, and my wolf never saw it as a threat. Quite the opposite. It was more like he could see the beast of my soul and she liked it.

"Josie, the bond is growing, and I know you feel it too. It's only going to get stronger. If you are planning to break our bond, I just ask you do it now and not later."

I stared at him feeling hurt and confused. Break our bond? Was that even an option?

He looked so vulnerable that it broke my heart. I was doing that to him.

I wasn't ready to tell him the truth about my pathetic life and how big a part of it he had always been.

"I don't want to make any decision today. It's still too new and confusing," I admitted.

In truth I was just scared. A big ole scaredy cat. Everyone in my life had let me down except him, but wasn't that just a matter of time? Were all these emotions from a lifelong one-sided crush I'd had on him, the bond, or were they somehow real? And how could I possibly know when they all seemed so mixed together?

He nodded his head sadly and then grinned. "Okay, so we have a snow day. No adulting necessary. What do you want to do with it?"

"I think I had enough time out in the snow yesterday. Can we just stay in and have a quiet day?"

"We can try."

"What does that mean?"

"The doghouse could get a little rowdy with all of us cooped up inside. And from the reports I don't think it's really safe to drive anywhere."

I shrugged. "We'll just make the most of it then."

I looked around the mostly bare room. There was no TV, no computer, there was absolutely nothing personal about this room.

Tyler noticed and gave me a sheepish grin. "Don't really live in here. What are you looking for?"

"I dunno. I was going to suggest a movie or something."

He kissed down my neck. "Or something," he mumbled.

I laughed, "Tyler."

"Fine. TV it is. Give me a few minutes. Just make yourself at home."

"Do you need any help?" I asked him.

Breakfast had been nice, but I found I really didn't like him out of my sight, especially after everything that had happened in the woods I was still feeling a little bit on edge.

"Sure, come on."

We walked down the hall and into another room. His scent was stronger there. This room had stuff everywhere and I could see that three people lived there.

"Hey," Pete said in a groggy voice from the only occupied bed. "Did you hear, classes are canceled."

"Yeah, I got the text. I think we're going to have a movie day in," he explained. "Just need to grab my TV and some stuff."

Pete gave a sad smile. "I guess I should say it's about time. Never thought you'd actually move out of here."

Tyler laughed. "Not sure I am yet. But gives us more space while Josie's here."

"So this is your actual room?" I asked him.

"They both are," Pete explained. "He just usually prefers to stay in here. We've been rooming together since freshman year. Brian too. He got up early this morning though. Probably went to Amber's."

Tyler shrugged. "He was making breakfast earlier. I didn't know classes were canceled at the time. Did you hear he's planning to mate Amber? They're officially petitioning their Packs for approval."

"Wow. I hadn't heard. Been busy lately and a little out of the loop. That's great though."

Amber had already told me that was their plan. It had sounded like a safe choice to me, a decision I would be more prone to make than her. Somehow our lives got all mixed it up. Here I was battling this spontaneous attraction from a true mating bond, and she was the one playing it safe. How did life get so turned around?

"Do you want some help with that?" Pete asked seeing Tyler disconnecting the large TV on his desk.

"Sure, that would be great."

"And you know, you're always welcome in here, right?"

Tyler snorted. "Yeah, I know. The bed's bigger in there though."

My head whipped around, and my cheeks burned.

"I didn't mean it like that. Just if we're going to hang out in there it's more room to stretch out." He laughed and gave me a sheepish grin.

"We could pull a couch in if you really want," Pete suggested.

"Not necessary," Tyler told him with a hint of warning in his voice that only made the blush spread down my neck and chest too.

Snuggled up with Tyler in bed all day sounded amazing, but I wasn't sure we were going to be watching too much TV if that was the case.

My body warmed all over remembering what he'd done to me, and what I'd asked him to show me to do to him last night. I had no idea what had come over me, but I'd never felt so powerful and in control of anything as I did with him.

It was like for the first time, all of my usual anxieties and need for order were put to rest. I loved it. I could easily become addicted to it and that both thrilled and terrified me.

Pete and Tyler moved the television down the hall refusing to let me help. I took a minute to look through Tyler's stuff. There was a picture of his family. I easily recognized them from memories I had of them from our childhood.

Another picture was of Tyler with a pretty girl with thick red dreadlocks. Somehow, I knew it had to be Karis. She popped up in a few other pics too, one of which that Damon guy was glaring at Tyler in the background.

The rest of his pictures looked to be him and some of the Delta Omega Gamma brothers.

The one common theme was Tyler's smile. He was happy here. Tim had told me that I should talk to him that he had easily chosen to walk away from everything to come here with his mate and that Tyler might surprise me. Seeing him like this in these photos I wasn't sure I could ask him to do that though. And if he did, that would mean dropping out of college and where would that leave us down the road?

Pete came back in and caught me snooping around.

"We've got it all set up in there," he told me.

"Thanks," I mumbled.

"You know, you're getting one of the best with him. There's nothing any of us wouldn't do for Tyler. He's genuinely a great guy and you must be pretty damn special to be mated to him."

I didn't know how to feel about that, so I muttered another 'thanks' and headed back to the other bedroom.

I already knew he was one of the good guys. Even as a kid he had been the best. But the man he had grown into was better than anything I had ever dreamed and certainly far better than I deserved.

Tyler was already laying on his back, his feet crossed at the ankles and one arm behind his head, the remote in his other hand.

He patted the bed next to him.

I closed the door behind me and snuggled down next to him.

"The other night you said Vampire Diaries was your favorite TV show. Should we binge watch it?"

"Have you seen it?"

"Never."

I bit my lip. "Okay, but you can't laugh or make fun of me for this."

"I wouldn't dare, but now you officially have me worried."

I shook my head. "They don't always show the wolves at

their best."

"It's make-believe, Josie. I think I can handle it."

To his credit, he lasted almost two hours.

"Josie, this is bullshit. You're trying to tell me that asshole Tyler is going to be the wolf shifter? He's a douchebag. I just can't."

I laughed. "He's redeemable much later. You're only a few episodes in. You have to stick with it."

"I'm a wolf named Tyler. I don't want that asshat associated with me."

My side hurt from laughing at him. "It's not you, it's just a character. I shouldn't have told you."

"I would have still struggled just because he has my name. I can't watch this."

He reached for the remote, but I grabbed it first. He rolled over me pinning me to the bed as I tried to keep it out of his reach.

"You promised to give it a try."

"I did try. It sucks."

"Tyler Anthony Nigel Klein, you take that back right now."

"Nope. I'm only speaking the truth."

I faked a gasp and shoved the remote underneath me.

"Oh, challenge on sweetheart."

My heart did a funny little flip every time he called me that.

When I tried to hide the remote, I hadn't really considered the predicament it could land me in.

Tyler's arms wrapped around me as he searched for the remote and he face planted right into my breasts.

I gasped, instantly turned on.

I might have been entirely innocent when I arrived here, but I had a feeling he was going to corrupt me thoroughly before I leave.

Tyler

Chapter 13

I hadn't meant to let things escalate. My plan had been to keep things light and easy for the day. I wanted her to relax and maybe even open up to me some more. She'd asked for one day a time and today could be all I got. I wanted to make the most of it, but I hadn't intended to complicate things further with sex.

I knew our bond was strengthening, but if she was leaving me behind, I didn't think that was a good thing. Still, I couldn't stop the need to be close with her.

My face was there before her breasts. What was a guy to do?

She gasped when I sucked her through the T-shirt she was wearing. I loved that she was still wearing my clothes. The fact is that she didn't have any of her own things here except that dress in my trash can that probably still smelled like Damon.

I growled and rubbed myself against her. I needed her to carry my scent, just mine.

Her hands fisted in my hair.

"Where is he?" a voice yelled from down the hall.

I sat up quickly. "Uh-oh."

Josie's face dropped. "Uh-oh?"

I double checked to make sure we were both decent just before the door flew open and Karis walked in. Damon was right behind her trying to pull her back out of the room as she swatted at him.

She glared at me and Josie growled.

I couldn't help the smirk that crossed my face. I settled back down next to her and pulled her into my arms to help calm her wolf.

Karis was no threat to Josie, but she also shouldn't have just barged in here like this.

"So it's true?" Karis demanded.

"Is what…?"

"Don't. I had to find out from Damon, Tyler. Why didn't you tell me?"

I sighed and cut my eyes down to Josie. "I've been a little busy, Kare."

"Well you can come up for air for five minutes to pick up the phone and tell your best friend that you found your one true mate."

I grinned. "Karis, this is Josie, my one true mate."

She squealed and threw herself into bed with us as she tackled Josie.

"Sorry," Damon said.

"It's fine."

At last I picked up the remote and turned her show up, but not before Damon saw it and laughed.

"Vampire Diaries?"

"Shut up, it's her favorite."

"Bet she's a Damon fan. Admit it, Josie, you're Team Damon, aren't you?"

I growled at him, but it only made his smirk grow.

I looked down and Josie blushed. She was definitely Team Damon.

"Not him," I complained, and she just shrugged.

Damon laughed. "All Damon's are awesome."

"It's just a coincidence," I argued.

She may like that Damon better but that had absolutely nothing to do with this one.

"Ohhh, wait, Tyler's the asshole. Oh, this is rich, and so much like real life," he insisted.

I groaned.

Josie chuckled.

"It's not funny," I told her.

"He wasn't exactly thrilled when I told him Tyler was the wolf."

"Vampires are so much cooler," Damon insisted.

"Says the wolf shifter," I reminded him, enjoying a momentary victory.

"I don't even know what you're talking about," Karis admitted.

My jaw dropped and then I started full belly laughing.

"You've never seen Vampire Diaries?" I asked her.

Karis shook her head.

I turned to Damon. "So why exactly do you know so much about this?"

"Shut up," he said and added just enough Alpha power to ensure I'd feel it.

I laughed harder.

"Are they always like this?" Josie asked Karis.

"Always," she assured her. "Welcome to my life."

"I get why you keep Damon around, he's your mate, but why put up with Tyler?"

"Hey," I protested. "Best friend designation."

Karis snorted. "Life would certainly be boring without him."

I winked at her, causing Josie to growl again.

"I'm so sorry," she said.

"Don't be. It's perfectly normal. It settles a lot after you seal the bond, but until then it can be hard. Do you have anyone to talk to about it?"

Josie shook her head.

Karis was sitting on the edge of the bed and somehow I felt like the intruder.

"Well, you do now. And I hope we can be friends, like real friends and not just tolerate each other the way these two do."

"Us? I'm slayed. Damon and I are great friends, right D?"

He snorted, rolled his eyes, and walked out.

"Love you, too," I yelled at his retreating back earning me his middle finger. "Love that guy."

Karis shoved me. "Be nice."

"I'm always nice."

"Except when Damon's around," Josie admitted.

I laughed.

"That really is just how they are. You get used to it and learn how to ignore it after a while," Karis assured her.

"I'm going to round up some lunch. Anything in particular you want?" I asked Josie, but Karis was the one that answered.

"Can you make cheesesteaks for us? Pretty please? Trust me, you will not be disappointed. Tyler's a great cook."

"Um, yeah, sounds good."

I shook my head. "Absolutely no good can come from you two being friends."

"You mean nothing good for you," Karis corrected.

I groaned as I got up and left them to get to know each other.

When I walked out into the common room, I wasn't surprised in the least to find everyone there. Snow days were always this way and usually I loved it.

There was a movie on the main TV and then the other two had different video games going. The younger guys had pulled out the beer pong table and day drinking had already begun.

I knew my time at the doghouse was getting shorter by the day. I would miss this more than anything.

The second I walked into the kitchen requests started flying.

"No," I yelled back. "I'm just making cheesesteaks for the girls."

"Yes!" Dylan cheered. "Your cheesesteaks are legendary."

I groaned, pulled out the ingredients, and started cooking.

Fortunately, Karis had suggested something quick and even with the excessive number of mouths to feed, I was done in half an hour. I loaded up four plates with sandwiches and chips, and then announced the rest was available.

I stepped out of the way before the wolves descended but had to laugh when our one panther beat them all to the front of the line.

Damon was talking to Hudson about the possibility he'd get drafted by the NFL next fall. It was a long shot but he'd had several scouts watching him closely throughout the season.

"We'll see. First I just need to finish out this semester strong and pray I don't even up on academic probation and blow my chances entirely next fall."

"Is it that bad?" I asked him.

"I'm managing okay. Just nervous. Math is not my forte."

"But it is Tyler's," Damon said. "I'm sure he'd be happy to tutor you."

"Anytime. Seriously. That's what brothers are for."

Hudson stared at me and then back at Damon. "Did you two just agree on something?"

I snorted and passed Damon two of the plates I was juggling.

"Look," I said pointing out the window. "Maybe hell really did freeze over."

They were laughing when I walked back to the room.

When I walked in, the girls instantly shut up and looked up at me.

"What are you two up to?" I asked.

"Nothing," they said in unison.

"Shit! I'm so screwed."

"And you're the best. Gimme," Karis said.

I held the plate back and handed Josie one of them.

"Back off, these are for us."

Her jaw dropped. "Tyler Klein, you better be messing me."

Damon walked into the room to rescue me just in time.

"Amore mio, this is for you."

She grinned and then pulled him down for a quick kiss.

"You are the best."

"What? I cooked them," I protested.

Damon took a seat on the end of the bed while I opted for the desk chair while we ate.

Josie took a bite and moaned. "Oh my gosh, this is delicious."

"I told you," Karis gloated proudly.

There was a comfortable silence while we ate, and I couldn't help but love every second of it. The most important people in my life were all in one room, yeah, that even included Damon, but only because he was important to Karis.

When we were done, Damon took Karis's plate and handed me Josie's.

"Can I talk to you for a minute?" he asked.

"Sure." I turned to Josie. "Are you good? We'll just be a few minutes."

"We're good," Karis said.

I rolled my eyes. "Are you good, Josie?"

She beamed up at me. "Yeah, I really am."

It wasn't easy leaving them. I felt like I was being left out, which was stupid because I wanted them to become friends.

"You holding up okay?" Damon asked as we got back to the kitchen.

"As good as can be, I guess."

"The guys told me you had some issues the other day. Something about Josie running off. Is everything cool now?"

"Honestly, I have no freaking clue. When we're together, things seem great."

"But…"

"D, she's flying home tomorrow and I don't know what to do."

"Shit. That's not good."

"I know."

"Are you going to seal the bond first?"

"I can't do that to her."

"If you don't, you're talking about an unresolved bond. Even I can feel your bond growing since I saw you the other day and you two were pretty cozy when Karis barged in. I've heard nightmare stories about unresolved bonds. That's not something you want."

"Yeah, well, I don't want her to leave tomorrow either, but I don't know how much of a say I get in this."

"I'm sorry man. That sucks. Did you ask her to stay?"

"Of course I did."

"She said no?"

"She didn't say anything. She just shook her head and ran out upset."

"That's what triggered the whole forest situation?"

I nodded.

I didn't particularly enjoy divulging this to Damon of all people, but despite everything, I trusted him and his advice on things.

Jackson walked in and stopped. "Damon and Tyler alone, together, and no bloodshed? This is a day for miracles."

I frowned and Jackson shut up and tuned in quickly when neither of us took the bait.

"What's wrong?"

"Just mating stuff. You know how that goes."

He groaned. "That madness is still too fresh. What's going on?"

Damon filled him in. I didn't mind because I knew Jackson was mated too and would understand more than most of my brothers possibly could.

"So, if she really insists on leaving, I guess my big question is, are you staying?" Jackson asked.

"I considered that," I admitted. "I was even going to talk to some of my professors today to see if remote classes for the rest of the semester would even be an option. Three months. I just have to get through three months and then I can graduate and follow her anywhere. But if I drop out of college now, what kind of mate would I even be?"

There it was. I'd said it aloud voicing my biggest concern of all. I couldn't lose Josie. I would willingly follow her anywhere she wanted to go. Hadn't I just been stressing out over the idea of returning to New York anyway? But if I didn't get that degree, it would limit my employment options, and then how would I support us?

This was far too big to screw up. I just wish I knew what the right path for us was.

Josie

Chapter 14

I really did like Karis. I hadn't expected to especially given how close she was to Tyler. But I genuinely liked her and could see us being friends.

"Okay, girl to girl, what do you think of our boy, Tyler?"

I bit my lip and she grinned.

Until that moment I had no idea I needed someone to talk to about this so badly.

"Truthfully? I've sort of known him since we were three. And even though I hadn't seen him since we were six, I have always had a weird thing for him. I never forgot him. So it kind of feels like none of this is real. I keep waiting to wake up and find it was all just a dream."

"I had no idea you two knew each other."

"I guess we really don't. I mean we were just kids. He didn't even know who I was when we met the other day, but I knew exactly who he was."

"That's so sweet. But he's an idiot."

"I'm pretty sure he figured it out on his own, but it, well, it hurt when he didn't recognize me right away."

Karis nodded. "I'm not surprised. The bond can really screw with your emotions and make you feel like you're going insane. They don't have to be rational. It's okay. That's normal. I'm guessing you guys were close when you were kids then?"

I nodded. "He was my best friend. We did everything together. He was also my first kiss even though he says that didn't count because we were five. But it counted to me."

"That's so sweet. What was he like back then?"

I shrugged. "Daring. He was so brave. Nothing scared him. He was always getting us into trouble or dragging me off on some new adventure. He was just as sweet and funny as he is now. He always makes me laugh."

"This is like fairytale level shit right here, Josie."

"I used to think so. My parents never stayed in one place for long. They just sort of go where the wind takes them."

"That's cool."

"It's really not. I didn't have a good childhood. I never felt safe. Everything was always out of my control, and it was so lonely. That's probably why I held on to Tyler's memory for so long. But I finally convinced them to let me stay with my aunt. She's been good to me, but we aren't exactly close either. In some ways I was more of a burden than anything, but I never caused any trouble. I always did everything asked of me and slowly I made a life I could count on there."

"Josie, I'm so sorry."

"Why? It's not your fault I had a shitty childhood. Tyler was always my one good memory. The one I talked to and confided my troubles to. Of course, he doesn't know any of that. I doubt he remembers, but just before my family moved from New York, I got the chance to tell him bye. That was a rare treat. We usually left so quickly there was never time for closure with people. Anyway, he told me not to worry, that when his wolf came in, he would find me and make me his mate."

"Oh my gosh! That's the sweetest thing ever and here you are together all these years later," she gushed.

I frowned and shook my head. "I grew up a long time ago, Karis. Stuff like that doesn't really happen."

"Open your eyes girlfriend, it is happening."

The door opened and Amber walked in. "What's happening?"

"Nothing," I said a little too quickly hoping Karis wouldn't say anything.

I'd just confided that to her in private. I had no idea what possessed me to tell her. I think I just really needed someone to hear it. Everything was happening so quickly and my head was spinning from all the crazy emotions that being near Tyler seemed to cultivate.

I hadn't meant to share that with her, but it had felt good to say it aloud.

The door opened again. I looked up expecting Tyler and Damon to return, but it was Jess and a couple other girls. Some I had seen around but really hadn't met them yet.

"Hey, we thought we heard a girls' night up in here," Jess said holding up a bottle of wine and passing cups around.

"Do any of you guys have a dampener around here?"

"Covered," one of the girls said as she plugged a device into the wall.

"Thanks, Tobi. You're the best. Josie, have you met everyone yet?"

I shook my head. "I know Amber, and Tim introduced me to Jess. That's about it."

"I'm Marie, Holden's mate."

"And that was Tobi. She's Jackson's mate," Karis informed me.

"Ember and Chad stayed home today," Tobi said rolling her eyes.

"And that's the whole crew since Brett and Jade moved, and Chase and Jenna rarely visit anymore," Karis said. "It's like a whole new generation."

"I don't graduate until May, so Jackson's been hanging out working on his Masters and busy starting up his own company," Tobi said.

"I can't even believe you're all leaving us soon. I mean Karis will be going back to Alaska. Tyler, Pete, and Brian are all graduating. Chad and Ember will stick around another year so he can finish his graduate program and then who knows where they'll end up. The ARC doesn't exactly have the best options for his residency," Marie said with a pout.

"We won't be that far behind them," Jess reminded her.

"I know, it sucks, like the end of an era is upon us."

Tobi snorted. "That wasn't dramatic at all."

I noticed Amber was sort of standing outside of the group and watching us but not really saying anything.

"Amber, come sit with me," I said hating thinking my friend was being left out. "Do you guys know Amber?"

"Sure. You're, Brian's girlfriend, right?" Marie asked.

Amber nodded but hesitantly came to sit next to me.

"They'll be mated right after graduation," I told them.

"Really?" Jess asked.

Amber nodded and her chin stuck out defiantly. "We've already petitioned our Packs and are just waiting for approval. I don't think we're waiting for graduation if it comes through sooner."

"Amber that's great," Karis said. "Really."

But there was an awkwardness to the group, and I didn't understand why.

"How are you holding up, Josie?" Jess asked.

"Me?"

"Of course you. Tim told me you were struggling to accept the bond and planning to leave. Sorry, we aren't very good with secret's around here."

"You're leaving?" Karis asked.

The look in her eyes told me she didn't approve.

"Tomorrow," I finally managed to say.

"What? Does Tyler know?"

I nodded.

"She only came for a visit," Amber defended me.

"But you're mating. Do you have any idea what that's going to do to him?"

"Forget him," Jess said. "I made that mistake for a year. It was horrible."

"She was like a ghost of herself just walking through the motions. I thought something terrible had happened to her, but it was the bond. That's not something I'd wish on anyone. I couldn't do it. I'm not saying I had it easy, just that mating is hard enough without making it even harder with distance."

"I've already bought my plane ticket. It's non-refundable. And I start my new job on Monday. What am I supposed to do? I can't just drop everything and uproot my life to stay here."

From the looks on the faces around me, that's exactly what they expected me to do.

"Of course you can't," Amber said rubbing my back and trying to be supportive.

Marie glared at her and I understood. Amber had a compatible mate and I wouldn't deny she was happy and in love. Did I love Tyler? Yes. I'd always loved him. Maybe when Amber and Brian sealed their bond she could understand, but right now there was no way Amber could possibly comprehend the merging of two hearts called together by a true mating bond.

It physically pained me to think about leaving him, but I didn't know what else to do.

Karis shook her head and there were tears in her eyes as she scooted off of the bed.

"You're going to destroy him," she said as she started to leave the room.

"Karis, stop. Don't be like that," Jess begged. "We've all been there and know how crazy the bond can make you. Have a little faith. They'll figure it out just like we all did."

"I just can't stand to see him upset or in pain. He's my best friend. I just want him to be happy. I can see how happy he is with you, and you're just going to rip that away from him."

"Maybe he'll go too," Tobi whispered.

"That wouldn't surprise me," Marie said. "But he only has three months left."

"That's not so bad," Jess said. "Even if you have to be apart for some of that. I mean I survived a year and Tim and I didn't resolve our bond in that time and it almost killed me, so word of advice… seal the bond before you leave."

"Unless she doesn't choose him," Amber said.

Karis's hand moved from the door as she walked back to us. "Not choose him? He's her true mate. Why wouldn't you choose him? You said you've wanted him since you were kids."

I hated the feeling of being put on the spot like this. It made my cheeks burn.

"Is that true, Josie?" Amber asked. Then she gasped. "Is that who you named your teddy bear after?"

"Explain," Karis said as I shot Amber a traitorous look.

"She has a stuffed bear she used to talk to all the time growing up. She called it Tyler Teddy. Of course we had a big ceremony after we graduated high school to burn that thing and move on, but I know that wasn't easy for you."

"You burned Tyler?" Karis asked.

I looked back and forth between her and Amber and shook my head.

"We burned a lookalike. I just couldn't do it," I confessed.

"What? Why?"

"I can't explain it. I needed to let go, but I couldn't quite bring myself to do it."

"Have you always known he was meant to be yours?" Tobi asked.

I shrugged. I didn't want to talk about it. It was so screwed up. A young girl's fantasy and nothing more. At least it hadn't been anything more, until I came here.

"You don't have to answer that," Tobi said. "But I'm curious. You said you have a new job waiting for you. What kind of job?"

"She's a nurse," Amber said proudly.

I nodded. "I graduated in December. I've been working part time just as needed and finally got hired on full-time.

"But nurses can work anywhere," Marie blurted out.

"You would think, but it took me months to secure this position."

"Couldn't hurt to check out the market around here, could it?"

I hadn't even considered that. I knew nurses could work anywhere, but it literally hadn't dawned on me to apply anywhere else and I'd put the time and effort into securing a job close to home.

"Stop pressuring her," Amber said. "Josie, you know I'd love for you to stay, but I know you. Are you sure you can just pack up and move here on a whim?"

And that was the thing. I knew I could, because I was my parents' child and the apple never falls far from the tree. That was the real reason I couldn't concede to stay. I couldn't live like them.

Amber hugged me. "You don't have to make a decision right now. And you don't owe anyone an explanation."

I nodded.

"Except Tyler," Karis pointed out.

I sighed. “We’re working on it. I don’t want to hurt him, Karis.”

She huffed. “I know you don’t.”

Karis walked over and hugged me as tears pricked my eyes.

“Mating sucks,” Jess said with a laugh.

“It totally sucks,” Marie agreed.

Soon all five of them were hugging me. It made me feel like I was somehow a part of something for the first time in my life. Even though they didn’t all agree with my plans, they were being supportive and trying to help me navigate through this crazy time in my life.

“Okay, okay. We’re here to support you,” Karis said. “Just please don’t hurt him. He’s not always as tough as he appears.”

I nodded. “I know.”

It surprised me that I wasn’t jealous of Karis. I had been when I first met her. I mean, how could I not? She was Tyler’s best friend, and that felt a bit like my role in his life, or at least it should have been.

She was very protective of him, and I appreciated that.

The last thing I ever wanted to do was hurt Tyler. I knew it wouldn’t be easy to go home and leave him behind, but I had to believe we could make it work. If we were truly meant to be together, then it had to work.

A part of me wanted to swear that I’d do absolutely anything to be with him and make him happy. But I wasn’t sure I could compromise the foundation of my own principles to do that, regardless of whether anyone understood them or not.

“You need to talk to him,” Karis finally said.

“I will,” I promised not just her, but myself too.

“Before you leave,” Jess added.

I laughed and relaxed just a little.

“Before I leave,” I agreed.

Just then my phone dinged, and it gave me a sick feeling in my gut. I knew it was coming. The twenty-four-hour mark. It was time for me to check in to confirm my flight.

I picked up and opened the text.

ALL FLIGHTS ARE CANCELED.

"What?" I said aloud. I checked the weather and saw that snow was continuing to fall and the storm was expected to last up to forty-eight hours longer.

The news was reporting people stuck in airports for possible days as planes were grounded.

"What's wrong?" Amber asked.

"This storm. It's canceled my flight tomorrow. They don't expect to have planes back in the sky for a few more days."

Tobi snorted. "Now that is what I call fate's intervention."

"Looks like you have a few more days to figure things out," Marie said with a grin.

"Don't screw this up," Karis warned.

Tyler

Chapter 15

I loved that Karis, and the girls were getting to know Josie. I hoped they made her feel welcome here, but I didn't want to get my hopes up that she would change her mind and stay.

I started pacing the floor while my brothers settled in to play video games.

This sucked.

I only had today with her, and I wanted to make the most of it. I didn't want to be an ass and kick the girls out, but dammit, I wanted to spend every second possible with my mate.

"It's really coming down out there," Jackson said, watching out the window.

"I've never seen it snow like this here," Hudson agreed.

"It's California. I didn't even know it was possible," Pete said with a laugh.

"Not all California is sunshine and bikinis," Brian added.

"Clearly," Pete responded.

I usually enjoyed their bantering, but the snow only made me stress even more. I felt trapped and incapable of doing anything about it… much like how things were going with Josie.

The trapped feeling wasn't about her though, it was about her choices and how they were going to impact me too.

I'd already taken a few minutes to put out some inquiries to my professors, but I didn't actually expect to hear back from them anytime soon.

It was a snow day and I'm sure the last thing they were doing was working.

Karis walked into the room, and she walked over and hugged me. "You need to talk to that girl and soon. Do not let her get away."

"I'll never let that happen," I swore.

"Are you sure about that? Just go to her and fix this, Tyler."

I didn't want to admit that I didn't know how but was doing everything I could.

When I saw the other girls return too, I ran back to the room. Only Amber was there.

"She's in the bathroom. You should know, she's always had a thing for you. I didn't realize that was actually you until now. She's fragile, Tyler. And you have the power to destroy her. Please don't hurt her."

My mouth went dry and I nodded.

Destroy her? I was terrified she was going to destroy me.

Amber left the room just before Josie came out of the bathroom. I could see she had been crying or was on the verge of it.

I couldn't get to her fast enough as I pulled her into my arms and just held her. I breathed in her sweet scent letting it calm me.

"Are you okay?" I asked.

She laughed. "I'm fine."

"You've been crying."

"Not really."

I wanted to beg her not to leave tomorrow. How could I possibly protect her from the other side of the country?

Instead, I kissed her. It was a sweet kiss filled with promises that I hoped to God she let me keep.

"I missed you," I told her.

She gave me a look. "You were just down the hall, and it hasn't even been an hour."

I shrugged. "I still missed you."

"Well," she bit her lip nervously, "you might not be missing me again for a while."

My heart started to swell but I knew I couldn't get my hopes up that maybe she'd changed her mind. "How so?"

She sighed. "They're calling it the biggest blizzard of the century. All flights are grounded until further notice. I tried calling to rebook and they aren't even allowing that yet. I'm stuck."

I bit back a grin as my heart swelled with relief. She wasn't going home tomorrow. I had more time. Beyond that we'd see. A lot could change in a few days, they already had.

She gave me a scornful look but there was a smile tipping the corners of her mouth. She rolled her eyes. "It's okay to be happy about it," she finally said with resignation.

I picked her up and twirled her around the room.

"Best news ever!" I kissed her again. "Maybe it'll snow forever and I can just keep you locked away in my snow fortress." A memory hit me, and I grinned. "Hey, do you remember that big snow we had? I think we were about five. The whole city was practically shut down from it and since the humans weren't venturing out, your parents bundled us up and took us to Central Park."

"We went sledding and built that snow fort before they challenged us in a snowball fight," she said.

I nodded. "That fort held, because we'd built it together, Josie."

She stared up at me with her big blue eyes and nodded.

"Together, we can survive anything, sweetheart."

I pulled her close to me. I just needed to hold her.

"My parents were always doing ridiculous things like that," she finally said.

"What are you talking about? That was a great day."

"Sure that one was, because you were there."

I could sense there was a lot more she wasn't saying. I guided her back to the bed and laid down with her by my side.

"Tell me."

At first, I didn't think she was going to, and then she started to open up.

"I have a lot of great memories of our time together in New York, but if I'm being honest, they're the only good memories I have, until now."

"It can't have been that bad," I whispered.

She looked up at me with sad eyes. "I don't like to talk about it."

My wolf was starting to stir. Something was wrong and I couldn't help but imagine the worst. "You can tell me anything, Josie."

"I know," she said softly.

When I didn't think she was going to speak, I tried a different route. "Where are you parents now?"

She shrugged. "I don't know. I lost track of them a few years ago. They check in with Aunt Courtney every now and then, but I rarely hear from them anymore."

"I'm sorry," I said.

"Don't be. I asked them to stop calling. I hate hearing about their adventures."

"But why?" I asked. I couldn't imagine it.

I remembered her parents as being free spirits, naturalist, and so much fun. They were adventurist and let us get away with things my parents would have been livid over had they ever found out.

She sighed. "I don't expect you to understand. To others they were the fun parents, the best, but being their daughter sucked, Tyler. New York was probably the longest we ever stayed anywhere. We drove across the country and back a few times. Sometimes we'd stay in an area for a month or two, sometimes just a few days. Never anywhere long enough to actually meet people and make friends."

I stayed silent but rubbed her arm trying to encourage her to talk. I needed to understand where she was coming from if we were ever going to be able to move past it.

"There were times when I'd be left alone for days, weeks even. Usually at campgrounds where others were around to help if I needed it, but also remote areas where people largely kept to themselves. I was just a child. I had no business being stuck in a van for days all by myself, having to feed myself, and sit through storms all alone. It was terrifying at times. I never felt safe, and I learned quickly that I could never trust my parents. They simply didn't care. If I complained about it, they called me a sour puss and laughed. It took me years of begging them to stay put in one spot just long enough for me to actually go to school, something they didn't feel I needed, before they finally dropped me off at my Aunt Courtney's in the Virginia Pack to finish out middle and high school."

She paused as I was struggling to fully comprehend the trauma this had caused her, but I could feel her pain as real as my own.

"They called a lot at first, mostly to rub it in my face what they thought I was missing. In truth it only reaffirmed to me that I was better off without them. I don't expect you to understand any of this. But it's why the thought of packing up and moving here on a whim terrifies me so much."

"You think that would make you like them," I stated as the pieces started clicking into place.

She nodded. "I'm not the type of girl who shirks responsibilities, Tyler. I committed to that job and I've worked damn hard to secure it. If I just up and throw it all away just to be with you, how does that make me any better than them? They always told me to follow my heart."

"So you lay careful plans and ignore it instead," I said. She didn't have to admit it for me to know it's true, but she nodded against my chest.

"I'm scared," she whispered.

"Me too," I admitted. "But we're going to figure this out because losing you is not an option, Josie."

She gave me a squeeze. "I think I need to hear that more often."

I grinned down at her and then kissed her. "I'll be happy to remind you just how much I need you every second of every day."

I was growing hard being so close to her and her breathy gasp as she looked up at me told me she knew it too.

She smacked me playfully. "Tyler, we were having a serious conversation."

"Oh, I was being serious."

"You're a horndog," she said with a laugh.

"Only when you're around," I confessed, unashamed. "Hey, look at me Josie. One day at a time, right?"

She nodded.

"And now we have a few more days together to make the most of. One day at a time. We're going to get through this."

I just wished I knew what was waiting for us on the other side.

"Well one thing is for certain."

"What's that?" I asked her.

"I'm going to keep The Vampire Dairies to myself. You just don't fully appreciate it enough to share that with you anymore."

"Thank God!"

I kissed her and this time my hands roamed over her body making her squirm in my arms. I knew she was still a virgin, but I also knew from our time together that she was far from innocent.

She pulled back in protest making me frown.

"People have just been walking in here all day long. Behave yourself."

I groaned, jumped up and walked over to lock the door.

When I looked back, Josie was laid out on my bed with her long red hair fanned out around her. She took my breath away. I couldn't help but stare watching the blush of her cheeks grow and spread down her arms, and chest dipping beneath a fresh T-shirt of mine that she had changed into at some point.

It was the sexiest thing I'd ever seen, and I had an uncontrollable urge to mark her as mine right then and there.

"Mine," I growled as I stalked to her.

"You're crazy. Everyone in the house will hear," she whispered.

I had already spotted the dampener plugged into the wall. One of the girls must have brought it in because one minute I could hear them talking and giggling and in the next it was entirely quiet the way only a dampener could make happen.

"Dampener's still on. No one will hear anything outside of this room. You can scream as loud as you want."

"That sounded rather ominous, Tyler."

She was nervous. It was cute.

I had promised myself I would take things slow with her, but I wasn't sure I'd be able to keep that promise. I needed her naked and wrapped around me so badly.

I started at her ankles and kissed my way up her body, removing clothes as they got in my way and careful to avoid her sweet spot and her breasts as I burned a path up her body to capture her lips.

Her chest was rising and falling heavily; her body was pink all over; and I knew from my caresses her entire body was strung tight with desire.

"What are you doing to me?" she moaned.

"Worshipping every inch of you," I assured her.

She didn't protest so I didn't stop.

I kissed her breathless and while she was fully focused on that, I touched her at last. She was hot and ready for me already. Her body was strung so tight I thought she was going to explode in an orgasm with the first swipe of my fingers.

"Tyler," she gasped, holding on to me for dear life.

She was so close and ready. It would be easy to take her virginity right then. She likely wouldn't even feel the pinch of pain that could come with her first time.

I got so caught up in the wonders of watching her that I missed my opportunity, but what a show it was.

"You're so close, love. Just let go."

She stared up at me with so much trust in her eyes that made my chest puff out with pride. She had confided in me that she hadn't felt safe as a child and had lost trust in her own parents. That told me a lot. I was certain she didn't trust easily, yet she was trusting me.

I never wanted to let this girl down.

As she came to a peak, I held her in awe, never wanting to let her go.

This time when I kissed her it was gentle and loving.

"You're going to make it very hard for me to leave here, maybe even just leave this bed."

I smirked. "I like the sound of that."

She sobered quickly as she frowned, and I could feel her pulling away. I not only recognized the signs now, but I had a little better understanding of the why. It wasn't going to be easy, but at least gave me possibilities.

Josie

Chapter 16

Tyler made my head swim. The things he could do to me with his hands and his mouth were insane. I was a little worried about having actual sex with him. I just couldn't imagine how it could feel any better than this.

I tried to reciprocate and use the tools he had taught me to please him, too, but he brushed me off and I didn't know why. I'd never been intimate with a guy before. Never. I hadn't even kissed any other guy. Tyler was it for me and I wanted to make him feel as good as he made me feel.

"You're way overdressed," I pouted.

He kissed my shoulder. "I can literally hear your stomach rumbling."

My cheeks heated with embarrassment, the redheaded curse striking again.

"Maybe I'm just hungry for you," I said trying to sound sultry and failing miserably. I burst out laughing. "That was terrible."

He laughed along with me.

Admitting my shortcomings to him didn't embarrass me at all. It was the oddest thing, but I felt comfortable enough with Tyler to confess things I had never told anyone.

Telling him about my parents had been cathartic. I was glad he knew and just maybe he could understand where I was coming from now. It wasn't that I didn't want him because I did. I just didn't want to start our life with me giving up everything for him.

"Anything sound good for dinner?"

"Are you kidding? You've been spoiling me all day with great food. Did you really cook it all yourself?"

"Scout's honor," he said. This time he held up all three fingers.

I rolled my eyes and laughed at him.

"I really do cook. You can come out and watch if you don't believe it."

"Maybe I will."

"Okay, get dressed and come on. We're doing this."

I froze and looked around. "I don't actually have clothes here, Tyler. All of my stuff is at Amber's."

He shrugged. "What's mine is yours. Help yourself."

I groaned. "I love having your scent all over me, but it would be nice to wear clothes that actually fit again."

He frowned. "Fine, I'll see if Brian will run over and get your stuff for you. He's feeling bad for being an ass before he knew you were my true mate." He stopped and looked at me. I could feel his nerves. "That is, if you want to stay here. I'm not stopping you from going back to Amber's if you'd rather. I know you came to spend time with her."

I kissed him. "I'd rather spend time with you. I, uh, I need to spend time with you, Tyler."

"Thank God," he said, kissing me again.

I relaxed into his arms and wondered if life with Tyler would always feel so good.

If we were going to make dinner, I knew things couldn't escalate though, so I pulled back and started rummaging through his bag to find something clean to wear. I probably should have taken a quick shower, but I really didn't want to wash away his scent just yet. I feared I might be a little addicted to it.

When I was dressed and ready, we left the room hand-in-hand. He made a quick stop by his other room to ask Brian about bringing my stuff over.

"Dude, you know there's like three feet of snow on the ground and counting, right?"

"It's over four now according to reports," Pete chimed in.

"No shit. Are you serious?" he asked walking over to the window to look out. Everything was white. "How did Damon and Karis even get here?"

"They don't live here?" I asked.

"No. They live in a cabin off campus. A few of the other brothers live over in mated housing. Some just choose not to live in the house," he explained.

"Maybe Damon will let us borrow the snowmobile," Amber told Brian.

He shrugged. "I'll see. If they know it's for Tyler, Karis might just make Damon hand over the keys."

"Let's go find out," Amber said excitedly.

Pete watched them leave and then sighed. "Thank you."

"What?" Tyler asked.

"Look, I love rooming with you guys, but those two have no consideration. Even my noise cancellation headphones can't drown out their make out sessions. I just want to scream and remind them I'm right here."

Tyler laughed, but I was horrified and embarrassed for my friend.

"Don't worry about it," Tyler told me. "They really don't care, Amber included. They've not been able to keep their hands off each other since they met sophomore year."

"It's true," Pete said. "And every year they seem to just get worse or I guess more comfortable in here. I don't mind if you guys want to hang out, but if that's all you're doing, then I appreciate you moving into the other room."

"We're not," I insisted.

Tyler laughed. "Well, that's not all we're doing."

He gave my hand a squeeze and pulled me closer to the window to look outside with him. Pete got up and joined us too.

"It's pretty, huh?" Pete said.

"It's beautiful," I agreed.

"I love the snow. We should let our wolves out and go for a run."

"Four feet of snow, Tyler. We'd be lucky if we didn't lose someone in that stuff."

Tyler shrugged at Pete. "I mean, we could stay close and just play in it."

Pete shook his head. "You're a child."

"And you can't tell me no, so let's do it."

"You're crazy," Pete argued, but he chuckled as he said it.

"Come on. We'll make the pledges join us even if the others won't. Being President of this place has to have some perks, right?"

"Uh, what about my food?" I asked.

"Can it wait an hour? We're going to lose sunlight soon and even I'm not dumb enough to go out after that."

"Fine," I said dramatically. "I can't even remember the last time I played in the snow."

Tyler froze and his wolf was set on edge.

"What is it?" I asked.

"If you're going out there, you can't leave my side, Josie. Not even for a second."

I knew he was remembering the last time I'd ventured out into the snow without him.

"I won't."

I took his hand tightly and gave it a squeeze.

"Okay then, let's do this."

"You're insane," Pete argued.

"You love me."

Pete shook his head, but my heart flipped in my chest. He was right. I did love him so how the hell was I supposed to leave him?

He tugged on my arm, and I shook off my worries and followed him.

Ten minutes later he'd somehow convinced all the brothers to join in.

The snow was almost up to the top of the railing, but the porch was big enough that most of it was still clear. We all piled out and onto it to look out across campus. Everything was quiet and covered in white.

Damon was giving Brian a quick lesson for the snow mobile before taking off with Amber. It looked like so much fun. She threw her arms up in the air and yelled as they drove off. I wondered if maybe Tyler could take me for a ride on it later. I didn't think it could hurt to ask. I'd never done anything like that before.

Several of the brothers started stripping out of their clothes and leaving them on the porch. The first three shifted and ran out into the snow prancing around and making paths while the others cheered them on.

Tyler was naked beside me. It should have been weird, but it wasn't. It felt like the most natural thing in the world.

He climbed up on top of the railing, gave some sort of battle cry and then leapt into the air. As he was pulling out of a flip in midair, he shifted with a roar and landed on the soft snow.

Everyone went nuts screaming and cheering.

"Did you see that?" one of the pledges yelled.

"No way!" Dylan added.

"He couldn't do that again in a million years," Hudson said.

"That was awesome," Tim agreed.

"I want to try it," Jess told him.

She started stripping out of her clothes. I averted my eyes, but not before noticing her mate certainly wasn't. Tim had the biggest grin on his face that I'd ever seen.

He helped her up onto the railing and gave her some pointers before she jumped. She didn't get high enough to flip, but shifted on her way back down as she dove into the mound of snow.

"Still cool, Jess," one of their friends said clapping for her.

"Way to go, Jessie," Tim cheered.

Tim stepped up next and belly flopped into the snow.

"Woo! That is so cold. Brr." Then he shifted, no doubt letting his wolf warm him.

Those still on the porch laughed.

Tyler's wolf showed up and rubbed against my leg.

Holden and Hudson shifted and raced out into the snow and through the trails Tyler and some of the others had formed. Tyler looked up at me and whimpered before taking back off into the snow.

I giggled and started to remove my clothes ready to join him.

"Shit," Damon mumbled and started ordering the boys to turn their backs to me.

"Really? No one turned for Jessie. We're shifters, right?" I teased.

"Jessie is bonded, and Tyler is in wolf form. We'd all prefer to keep our throats intact. It's just a bit of respect, Josie," he explained.

"Whatever," I said with a laugh as I climbed up onto the railing.

I'd been studying the others and had watched how Tyler had done it. I bent my knees and using my arms I leapt into the air as high as I could. I flipped allowing my wolf to shift as I came out of the loop. I landed in the soft fluffy snow with a light thud.

Those still in human form cheered. Tyler had been watching and his wolf howled in excitement.

I ran over to join him remembering my promise to stay with him.

For the next few hours, we ran around playing in the snow as our wolves got to know each other. Every now and then he would rub up against me or sneak in a lick. It excited my wolf and made her more playful than I could ever remember as she pranced around and pounced on Tyler or into the snow.

I couldn't ever remember having a better time. I was carefree and happy, but it didn't scare me. There was nothing wrong with having fun. Sometimes I struggled with that because I had always associated fun with my parents. But I was still on vacation, and it was exactly the kind of thing I should be doing.

By the time we started winding down, I was exhilarated. As promised, I had stayed with Tyler the entire time. One by one the others had joined us and it had just been the best time I could ever remember having.

Tyler hung back as the others started to shift and change leaving the two of us as the last to walk back up to the porch and shift.

I grinned. "Did you plan that on purpose?"

"What?" he asked.

"Damon said you wouldn't be happy with me naked in front of your brothers before I went to shift."

He shrugged. "I'm dealing with it. He's been through it and understands that stuff like that isn't easy for me right now."

"Really? I mean we're shifters. I don't particularly like being naked in front of others. Heck, I've even skipped mandatory pack runs to avoid it, but I'm not going to destroy my clothes to avoid it either. I wouldn't have wanted to miss out on this for anything."

He pulled me into his arms and kissed me.

"They were just showing a little respect and I'm glad you joined in because that was so much fun."

"It really was."

My stomach grumbled and he groaned.

"But I didn't mean to be so long. I need to get you fed."

"I'm fine," I protested.

"You're hungry."

I laughed, feeling bold. "Oh, I'm pretty sure I'm always hungry when you're around."

He cursed under his breath looking torn on what to do next.

Finally, he sighed. "Food first. You're going to need your strength for that."

I gulped hard and froze in place.

He sniffed the air and grinned at the smell of my arousal. It wasn't like it was something I could hide from him.

"Fast food."

Before we walked back inside we heard the purr of an engine. I looked up to see Amber and Brian returning with my things.

He parked in front of the house and jumped down.

"That was so fun. You guys should definitely try it."

I looked up at Tyler hopefully. "Later."

"What the hell happened here? The beautiful snow is destroyed," Brian complained.

"We had a little fun while you were gone," I explained.

"Wait, you played in the snow?" Amber asked.

"Yes. It was so much fun."

"You should've seen her jump off the railing, flip, and then shift in midair. It was perfect," Tyler gushed.

"Not quite as good as yours but I didn't wipe out as bad as some of the others."

"Sweetheart, you didn't wipe out at all."

I shrugged.

Amber's mouth gaped, but she had tears in her eyes as she pulled me in for a hug.

"I am so proud of you," she whispered. "I wasn't too sure about this pairing," she said pulling back and pointing between Tyler and me. "But I think he's really good for you, Josie. He's pulling out sides of you I've attempted to reach for nearly a decade."

I groaned. Amber was always on the dramatic side.

"I'm serious, Jo. You just seem so much lighter with him, like all the heavy stuff is gone."

I shook my head. "Not gone. It's still there, just not as unbearable."

Tears spilled from her eyes as she hugged me again. "I just worry about you so much. And I love having you here even if I have to share you with him." Then she turned to Tyler. "She's tough, but she's also a lot more fragile than she lets on, especially where you're concerned. You hurt her, and I swear I will slit your throat in your sleep."

Tyler

Chapter 17

As I made dinner for everyone in the house with Josie insisting on helping, I couldn't stop thinking about her conversation with Amber. I should have been appalled by the blatant threat she had issued towards me, but instead all I could do was worry about why.

Why had she felt the need to say that?

Why would she think I would ever purposefully hurt my mate? If anything, I was more terrified she was going to hurt me when she left… not hurt, destroy me.

Why did she think Josie was so fragile? Did it stem back to what she had told me about her parents?

I thought I knew my mate well, but now I felt like there was a lot more catching up needed.

Since I was distracted and feeding a small pack of people, I went with a simple spaghetti dinner. Well, I couldn't quite muster up simple. They complained if there was no meat in a meal, and I knew Josie could use it too, so I made a basic meat sauce using a jar sauce that I doctored where I would have made everything from scratch if I'd had the time and the ingredients on hand. It wasn't my best, but it would do.

My priority had shifted from impressing Josie with my culinary skills to just wanting to get her alone and figure things out.

It took a lot longer to get us to that point than I expected because it turns out my mate was a natural nurturer. She played the part of hostess to perfection and somewhere in the midst of our snow-time fun she'd become a piece of the doghouse. I wasn't even sure if she was aware of it, but I felt the change all around me. They had accepted her, and she had them.

It made my heart overflow.

"You're pretty amazing," I told her as she dished out spaghetti and served my brothers and their mates.

She blushed and smiled but didn't say anything.

When everyone was served, I thought we could finally sneak off to my room, but instead, she handed me a plate, took one for herself and then walked into the common room and sat on the floor near the fireplace next to Karis.

While I wanted her all to myself, I couldn't deny how much I loved seeing her comfortable in the doghouse and especially with Karis.

I sat down next to her and ate with a smile on my face.

The guys talked, laughed, and teased her. She gave it back to them with equal measure. It felt like the most normal day of my life, and I wished every day could be as simple as a snow day.

*****

It was dark and late before we finally said goodnight and retreated to my room. Josie was yawning and I was ready for sleep. It was the last thing I wanted, but my first priority would always be her needs.

As soon as I shut the door and locked it, she stripped out of the clothes she was wearing and headed for bed.

I was so hard I could have pounded nails and I was pretty sure she was trying to kill me. I couldn't deny how happy it made me that she was becoming comfortable enough to sleep naked next to me without me having to strip her and satiate her to the point of exhaustion.

It was a simple thing but felt huge in my heart.

I followed her lead, removed my clothes, and climbed into my side of the bed. I grinned into the dark realizing we even had bed sides already.

She wrapped her body around me and rested her head on my chest.

I kissed the top of her head as I rubbed her back loving the way she relaxed further against me.

Why did life have to be so complicated when being with her was so easy?

"Today was a lot of fun," she told me in a sleepy voice.

"It was a perfect," I told her.

She giggled.

"What's so funny?"

I nearly jolted from the bed in shock as she wrapped her hand around me and started to stroke.

"If it were perfect, you wouldn't be poking me with this thing."

My entire body was strung tight, and I didn't know what to say. I tried to relax and enjoy it but keeping my hands to myself was proving difficult.

I loved how she was touching me, but I wanted so much more. I didn't just want, I needed her like I needed air to breathe.

I tipped her chin up to face me and then I kissed her as my hand roamed down her body.

I didn't stop her from touching me, but I desperately had to touch her too. She parted her legs and welcomed me as she greedily kissed me. The smell of her arousal was intoxicating, and it wasn't long before I was entirely lost in Josie.

The trick for me was making her come without her doing the same to me. I pulled her hand from me and pinned both of her arms above her head as I feasted on her breasts, as my hand brought her to the brink of an orgasm.

When I started to feel her tightening around me, I positioned myself over her and slowly took her. She was so tight, but I reached the final barrier of her virginity she was grinding her hips against me begging for me.

I wasn't sure I was going to last long yet I wanted her first time to be perfect.

As I pushed past that thin line, she cried out, but not in pain, in sheer pleasure as she constricted around me and started to shake.

I stilled long enough for her peak to pass, and then before she could come back down, I started to move within her.

I watched the shock and wonder on her face as she tried to recover while building to a second faster than I knew was possible. It was probably a good thing because I knew I wasn't going to last long. I was too worked up already from her playing with me first.

My canines started to elongate, and I wanted nothing more than to fully make her mine, but I knew we still had some heavy things to resolve before I could do that to either of us.

My wolf wasn't happy about it, but I pushed him back, determined to stay fully in the moment.

"Look at me, Josie."

Her eyes opened wide. They were a little hazy and her hair was a mess. She was so beautiful in mid-passion that it made my heart swell.

"You are mine," I told her and then I kissed her breath away until I was so close that sweat broke out on my brow and I had to pull back to catch my own breath.

She was so close. It took every ounce of restraint for me to wait for her to finally reach her release point. The second she started tightening around me, I couldn't hold out any longer and let myself go and collapsed on her and rolled, careful not to squash her.

She was panting and her eyes were heavy.

"Wow."

I grinned. "Wow."

She was quiet for a bit as her body started to settle.

I trailed feather light kisses across her cheeks and lips. If I hadn't known it before tonight, I knew without a doubt now that she was the most precious thing in the world to me.

"Are you okay?" I asked her softly.

She rolled to her side and stared in my eyes. I couldn't read them. I had no idea what was going through that head of hers and it was killing me not to know.

Was she freaking out?

Did I hurt her?

Was she as happy as I was?

She raised her hand and caressed my cheek. I leaned into her palm, craving her touch.

"I'm yours," she conceded. "But you're mine, too."

Relief washed over me as I smiled so big it hurt. I kissed her again. I didn't rush it, but the passion of earlier wasn't there either.

Instead, it was replaced with a promise of a future. I still had no idea how we were going to get through the next three months, but somehow, we were going to make it work.

As I thought about the future I couldn't help but think of Josie all big and round in the belly pregnant with my child.

That beautiful picture turned rancid in my gut.

"Shit!"

"What?" she asked. I could feel her panic as clearly as if it were my own.

"I didn't use a condom, Josie. Shit! I've never done that before."

I wasn't ready to be a father. Someday, but not now.

"Oh, is that all?"

"Is that all? Are you telling me you're okay with me getting you pregnant?"

She snorted and shook her head. "I'm on the pill, Tyler. It's fine."

My heart was still racing as I collapsed back down onto my pillow, unsure if I was relieved or pissed. I thought she'd been a virgin.

"Why the hell are you on the pill?" I blurted out.

Her cheeks pinked and she shrugged.

"Josie, why are you on birth control?"

She blew out a long breath. "Because I was an accident. My parents were careless and didn't protect themselves and then there I was. Twenty-some years later and they still haven't figured out how to be parents. I'll never let that happen, Tyler."

"You don't want kids?"

"I don't want a surprise baby. So when I turned sixteen and boys started noticing me some, I got on birth control. I didn't ever want to be put in a position like that. I've never really needed it, until now, but it just makes me feel better that I'm doing something proactive to protect myself."

It broke my heart that they had hurt her so badly. I still struggled to imagine her parents as the monsters that would hurt her, but even my six-year-old self could remember thinking they were cool and fun, but also immature and sometimes dangerous.

My mind tended to grace over the bad stuff in my life and hold on to the positive memories, but if I really thought about it, I could remember.

I held her tightly to me. Hating them for what they had done to her.

"You shouldn't have had to think about that. And I shouldn't have been so careless. I'm sorry."

She peeked up at me and grinned. "You are not apologizing for *that.*"

I barked out a laugh. "That's not what I meant."

"I know what you meant, Tyler."

"I've never had sex unprotected before. Not ever. I couldn't with anyone but you. I never want to purposefully hurt you or put you in a position that makes you uncomfortable."

She smiled and brought my lips back to hers.

"You most definitely did not make me uncomfortable. Not at all. Yes, we probably should have had this conversation before, but I knew we were okay. I'm not worried about it."

I hugged her. "I hate that they made you feel like you had to."

She shrugged. "They're my parents and I guess in some weird way I love them, but they've taught me everything I don't want in life, Tyler."

I nodded still wishing I could go back and keep her safe and with me all those years ago. It was my job to protect her and for fifteen years I'd failed her.

"Hey, what's wrong?" she asked.

"Nothing," I lied. "Nothing at all."

She planted a kiss on my chest.

"I can feel something's wrong," she whispered.

I eased up my hold on her so she could look up at me.

"I hate that you had to go through all of that alone. I should have been there, Josie. I should have protected you."

Tears filled her eyes. "You did. More than you can possibly understand."

I had no idea what she was talking about, but it broke my heart to see her cry.

Without another word I held her as she cried herself to sleep. It wasn't how this night should have gone, yet somehow, I felt better afterwards. Like she had been brewing those tears for a long time and was finally safe enough to let them flow.

Josie

Chapter 18

I felt like an idiot for crying myself to sleep after having sex for the first time. I couldn't even imagine what Tyler must be thinking and so I laid there pretending to sleep a little longer not yet ready to face him.

He had been wonderful. It was all so much better than I ever could have imagined. I could feel my muscles in my legs were a little sore this morning, but in a good way. Overall, I hadn't felt any pain like Amber had warned me about after she'd given her virginity away in the backseat of the quarterback's car in high school.

She had told me it would be awkward and painful at first, but if you weren't with a clueless idiot who had no idea what he was doing then it got better later. She had even suggested I just get that part over with, but I had never been able to make myself do it. Now I knew why—I had been waiting for Tyler.

I bit my lip. He'd definitely been worth the wait and now that I knew what to expect, it only made me crave more of him.

"I know you're awake," Tyler teased kissing each of my eyelids.

I squirmed and moaned, not ready to wake up and face him.

"I can hear you're hungry. I'm going to go find you some food."

I giggled. "Why are you always trying to feed me?"

I opened my eyes just in time to see that grin I loved so much.

"It makes me feel good to care for you and I'm good with food so it's something I can do," he admitted.

"Maybe there's something I need more than food this morning." I gave him a wicked grin as I pulled him to me for a kiss.

He smiled against my lips but, much to my disappointment, he didn't deepen the kiss.

"So are we okay?"

I looked back at him sensing just how concerned he was.

"I think so."

"You're not too sore or upset still about last night?

I blew out a breath. "I'm sorry I cried on you last night. It's just that these damn mating hormones are making me crazy."

"You can cry on my shoulder anytime you need, Josie. That doesn't bother me. I just need to know that you're okay, and then that we're okay."

"I actually feel better than I have in a long time. And I hope we're okay," I said starting to feel a little nervous that maybe he was looking for an out.

But he relaxed and smiled. "Okay. Breakfast or…" his hand trailed up my thigh and I knew exactly what I wanted.

"I don't need breakfast," I whispered.

*****

When we finally did come out of that bedroom after multiple orgasms, a shower, and real clothes, we walked into the main room holding hands and laughing. Everyone went quiet and stared at us.

"What are you assholes staring at?" Tyler asked.

"It's damn near noon," Damon pointed out grumpily.

Karis laughed. "We stayed over and slept on the floor. Ignore him."

"Why didn't you go home?" Tyler asked.

"That snow is pretty deep. Too deep to run back, and too cold to ride that far back."

"Why didn't you just tell me? We'd have made accommodations. You could have had my bed in with Pete and Brian."

"Jackson and Tobi stayed over too and called dibs first," Karis explained.

"You both look exhausted. We're going to make some lunch and hang out in here for a while."

"We are?" Tyler asked me.

"We are," I confirmed. "Why don't you guys go take a nap. You can take our bed, uh, Tyler's bed," I corrected, feeling the heat rising in my cheeks.

"Yeah, that's fine," Tyler finally conceded. "But you might want to change the sheets first on *our* bed."

I gasped and then smacked him across the gut.

Damon laughed.

"There's clean ones in the closest," he said as I grabbed his arm and dragged him away in embarrassment.

Some of the other guys were listening in and laughed too, but when I glared at them, they looked away and refrained from commenting.

Tyler gave me a sheepish grin and kissed me.

"Get a room," Brian teased as he and Amber walked in.

"Can't, she just gave it away to Damon and Karis."

I groaned and hid my face against his chest. His arms wrapped around me and just held me. I felt so safe in his arms like nothing bad could happen while Tyler was there.

"We almost came in and crashed with you guys last night. It was a full house around here."

"I think everyone but Chad and Ember was here. It's like all of Delta Omega Gamma decided it was a good idea to get snowed in together but no one considered the logistics of it," Amber grumbled.

"There's rumors that both Theta and the Panthers are coming to crash here for the day since classes are obviously canceled once again," Brian said.

Pete walked in and made himself a cup of coffee as we all stood around the kitchen talking.

"Heard half of campus is out of power now, including mated housing. Jackson's taking the snowmobile over to pick up Chad and Ember and bring them back here. They have an airbed they're bringing, not sure what you want to do with everyone. It was pretty packed last night," Pete said.

Tyler groaned. "I'll figure something out. If we lost power here we may all be dragging mattresses out and sleeping in the main room. At least we have a fireplace. I can't even imagine living in the dorms with no heat."

Pete shrugged. "I imagine most will just take to their fur. We'll get through it."

"You guys are just lucky I keep this place well stocked."

Brian snorted. "Can you even imagine if we ran out of food?"

"I don't even know if the cafeteria is open," Pete said. "It could be out of power too."

"Well at least all classes are canceled again today," Amber said as she linked an arm through mine and pulled me away from Tyler. "And we get Josie a little longer."

Tyler smiled down at me. "The snow can stick around forever then."

I groaned and shook my head. I'm starting a new job in Virginia in just six days. I was already getting anxious about whether I'd even be able to make it home in time.

"Unfortunately, it's supposed to warm up tomorrow, like into the sixties," Pete informed us all.

"I predict campus will flood," Brian said.

Tyler laughed. "That would be some shit. We'll need to watch the basement for any signs of that."

"So, what are you making us for lunch?" Brian asked.

I laughed. "Is Tyler the only one that cooks around here?"

"No, he's just the best," Pete explained. "Most of us eat around campus at the cafeteria or the café."

"Or in town. Jack's is pretty good and it's within walking distance. There's a few others along that strip of town too," Brian added.

"But Tyler really is a great cook," Amber told me.

"I've noticed," I said, watching his face light up from my praise.

He winked at me, but then spoke to Amber. "Was that actually a compliment?"

She groaned. "I won't make a habit of it. I'm just hungry. Mostly he's an annoying ass, but now you're my friend's ass so that elevates you just a little."

He laughed. "Well, you've always been my friend's ass."

"Watch it," Brian warned.

I just smiled and shook my head.

"You're all a bunch of assholes, and I'm hungry so what can I do to help speed this along?" Pete asked.

For the next hour the five of us talked and joked around while fixing enough food to feed a small army.

Growing up and watching television shows with Aunt Courtney, there was always this theme of warmth in the kitchen, family connections even, as if the entire world ran from a kitchen. I had never once experienced that in my life.

Well, maybe once. I had a faint memory of baking cookies once with Tyler and his mom when we were little. It was such a faded moment that I wasn't even sure it had really happened or if I had just imagined it.

I wasn't imagining this though. It was the most fun I'd ever had in a kitchen before and felt like I was living in one of Aunt Courtney's shows.

My use of the kitchen largely revolved around the microwave. Even in my apartment back home it was sparse and impersonal. That wasn't how this kitchen in the doghouse felt at all and it was completely unexpected. There were a bunch of frat boys living here and yet it felt like the homiest place I'd ever experienced in my entire life.

I looked around the room and I knew that was all Tyler's doing. Pete had even admitted that most of the guys ate on campus. This was a Tyler thing. It was his warmth and love that radiated throughout the kitchen and all through the house.

I had already learned he was President of the doghouse and I understood why.

"Hey, you okay?" Amber asked, putting an arm around my shoulder.

I rested my head on her shoulder.

"I'm great."

"He's really good for you, you know? I've never seen you so relaxed and so happy. It's nice. Are you sure you want to go back to Virginia, Josie?"

I gave her a sad smile. "I have to. I have a job waiting for me on Monday. You know that."

She sighed. "I know."

I could tell she wanted to say more, but I didn't want her to burst the bubble of another perfect day.

One day at time, I reminded myself.

There was a commotion outside and everyone was standing around looking out of the window. Tyler shook his head when he saw the snow mobile pulling up.

There was a squirrel riding on a piece of plywood that had been fastened to the snow mobile dragging along behind it piled high with stuff. Ember rode safely upfront with Jackson

The squirrel jumped down and ran into the house and straight for the fire to warm up. It wasn't just any squirrel, but the fattest squirrel I'd ever seen. He was so roly-poly that I half expected him to just topple over.

"You're an idiot," Tyler said with a laugh.

The squirrel looked up at him, grinned and started to chatter, though no one could understand a thing he was trying to say.

"A squirrel?" I asked.

"Chad," Tyler informed me.

"Chad's a squirrel? But he's a brother of the DOGs."

"He apparently started college back East somewhere and had pledged to Delta Omega Gamma at a human school. When he transferred here, they automatically put him in the doghouse," Pete explained to me.

"No one considered he wasn't a dog, just a frat boy." Brian laughed.

So far Pete had been the quiet one of the house, but he seemed relaxed and more open today. He seemed to know everything going on around the house.

By the time we finished up lunch, Jackson and Ember had unloaded a bunch of air mattresses, sleeping bags, and blankets. They were stacked in the corner of the room.

"We should check the basement and clean it. There's plenty of space down there for people to crash," Tyler suggested.

"Did anyone check on our pledges?" Jackson asked.

"Oh shit. No. I should probably do that," Tyler said. "If their dorms are out of power, can you go pick them up?"

"Sure. That was fun."

I'd seen the pledges in passing, but I hadn't really met them yet. I know there were eight of them this year. They were apparently the largest pledge class they'd had in several years. Tyler had tried to explain it all to me, but I'd given up trying to understand and told him it was all Greek to me. He had groaned and rolled his eyes.

A lot of the older guys were moving on or had recently. I hadn't met Brett, but they talked about him a lot. He was the old president and had graduated in December and moved out of the area. I wasn't sure where. Brett had groomed Chad to take over running the doghouse. They had co-led for a year, and then Chad only lasted one semester flying solo before he pawned it off on Tyler to finish out the year claiming it just wasn't for him.

"Well, lunch is ready if anyone's hungry," he informed everyone who had gathered around.

I walked back into the kitchen and started plating food to pass out to the brothers. I really enjoyed helping and talking with them all. It somehow made me feel like I was part of something. I certainly had never been a part of anything in the past. I hadn't even joined a club or anything in high school.

Now, here I was, mating the President of a fraternity. Tyler seemed born for the role too. It made my mind wander to what our life together could look like.

So far being with him had been unlike anything I'd ever experienced, and he was opening me up to new possibilities every day.

With Tyler by my side, I didn't feel alone, scared, or weak. Instead, I felt empowered and ready to try just about anything… within reason, because at the end of the day, the memories of what my life had been like growing up still weighed heavily on my heart.

Tyler

Chapter 19

I felt like an ass for not thinking about our pledges sooner. They were scattered across three dorms on campus and all of their buildings were without power.

I grabbed my phone and started calling the pledges.

Denny was first on my list.

"Hello," he asked, sounding a little nervous, maybe even downright scared.

"Heard you guys were out of power over there."

"Yes, sir."

"Why the hell didn't you call me?" I asked him.

"There's so much snow out there, we thought you'd order us to trudge through it and get to the house," he confessed.

I sighed. "I'm not that much of an asshole. Pack your things. Jackson's on the way to pick you up. Tell Josh to sit tight, He'll be taking one at a time."

"There's four feet of snow out there, Tyler. There's no way he can drive over here."

"Oh yeah? Watch and see. And pack some clothes and any pillows and blankets you need. Those things are scarce around here."

I hung up on him chuckling.

About half an hour later Jackson returned still pulling that board behind him. This time Josh was riding behind him, and Denny was holding on for dear life with all their stuff.

I stepped out on the porch laughing.

"What the hell are you doing?"

Jackson grinned and shrugged. "Faster this way."

"Denny, get inside and warm the hell up by the fire."

His teeth were chattering but the kid was grinning. "That was awesome!"

Jackson took back off as I made the rest of the calls to alert the others. Soon Bryce, Aiden, Cody, Kipp, Tanner, and Evan were all at the house safe and sound as they warmed up next to the fireplace.

"Thanks, Ty. You have no idea how cold it is over there," Aiden said.

"The guys on my floor were so jealous when Jackson rolled up to the door," Bryce said proudly.

"DOGs take care of their own," Tim told them.

"Damn right we do," Dylan added.

"Finn, Asher, Jamie, can you three come down to the basement with me to get started cleaning up?"

"We cleaned it on Sunday," Kipp insisted. "It's good."

"We were pretty thorough," Tanner said.

"It was nasty down there," Cody complained.

"Who made you guys clean?" I asked. I knew it hadn't been me. I was still in shock and dealing with the Josie and the mating call at that time.

"No one," Denny said proudly.

"You seemed pretty stressed, so we wanted to do something to help," Evan explained.

"This I gotta see," Jamie said jumping up.

Finn and Asher joined us without complaint.

When I saw the basement, my jaw dropped.

"Holy shit! When they say clean, they mean squeaky clean," Finn said.

"I can't believe I'm saying this, but I'd sleep on that floor." Asher sounded as shocked as I felt.

The basement was our party room. It housed the bar, a pool table, a beer pong table, and several old couches. We had a killer stereo system and even a dance floor. We only used it for party nights otherwise it was so disgusting no one ever really wanted to spend time down here.

I slowly walked back upstairs feeling a little shocked.

"Well? How did it look?" Jackson asked.

"It's spotless. Absolutely spotless."

The pledges high fived each other, proud of themselves.

Josie sat in the corner laughing with Ember and Amber. Jess and Marie were talking nearby and occasionally would join into whatever the girls were laughing about.

I stood there just watching my mate. She looked so relaxed and happy. She looked like she belonged there, because she did.

There was a commotion outside. We all moved to the porch as a stream of girls pushed their way through the mounds of snow.

"Panthers?" I asked.

I turned back to see Kian blanch and slowly back out of the room and down the hall, no doubt going to hide.

"What are you ladies doing here?" I asked as Ayanna, the leader of the Panther house stepped onto my porch. She was in her sixth year at the ARC finishing up her masters, but still in full control of the Panthers.

"We lost power. Even if you lose it here, you have the fireplace and plenty of warm bodies," she said with a purr.

She held out one perfectly manicured finger and I knew she was about to suggestively run it down my chest.

I growled in warning and saw the surprise in her eyes.

"Not you too," Chloe whined.

"What are you talking about?" Ayanna asked her.

"Only one reason I know of that would cause a man like Tyler to not want to be touched. You found your mate."

I couldn't stop the grin that crossed my face.

"And if you can keep your hands to yourself, you can come in and meet her."

"She's here?" Ayanna asked, a little surprised.

"Yeah."

"We're freezing, Ty. Please let us come in," one of the other girls said.

I was torn because while I just said they could, I also knew that it made Kian very uncomfortable to have them around and he shouldn't feel awkward in his own home.

"Yeah, fine. Come in," I finally said. If their power was really out, then I couldn't stomach turning them away.

As they started walking in, the Theta girls rounded the corner and joined them.

"Now what are you ladies doing here?" I asked.

"Heard there was a party at the doghouse." Mila asked.

"Who the hell told you that?"

"Fine, no one. We were just hoping. We're tired of being stuck in our house and it's so cold. We made it here, let us stay, Tyler," she whined.

"Come on, but I'm warning you all, the Panthers are already here and I don't want any trouble. Are we clear?"

"Yeah, fine. Just open the bar and turn on some music and we'll have a little fun. It's a snow day. There's no classes, we're young and wild, this is exactly what we're supposed to be doing."

"Oh yeah, what's that?"

"Having fun, Tyler. You do remember what that is, don't you?"

She stepped up into my personal space.

"Don't," I warned.

We walked inside.

"What crawled up your butt and died?" she asked.

"Found his mate. What else?" Chloe told her. "Are you guys out of power too?"

"No," Mila said. "Just bored and looking for some fun." She turned to me with big sad eyes. "Did you really find you mate?"

"I did."

"Your true mate?"

"Wouldn't settle for anything less."

She sighed. "What is it about this place? It's like everyone here is cursed to find a mate."

"Cursed? We consider it blessed," Holden told her grabbing Marie around the waist and cuddling her close to him. He kissed her neck making her giggle.

The Pledges all perked up quickly seeing our new arrivals.

Ayanna stood over Josie. "Who are you?"

"Hi. I'm Josie," she said innocently.

"That one's mine, Aye, mess with her and you'll deal with me."

Ayanna rolled her eyes. "Whatever. We'll be in the basement for anyone wanting to join us."

"Do not make a mess. People are going to have to sleep down there," I yelled at their retreating backs.

I didn't have to turn around to know my girl had gotten up and walked over to me. I could feel her behind me.

"Um, is everything okay?" Josie asked.

I didn't particularly like having a houseful of unmated males with her there, but they were my brothers, and I knew they wouldn't dare lay a hand on her. So anytime my panic started to rise I just had to remind myself that she was okay, and I was just being ridiculous. But now a house full of catty women made me equally uncomfortable because they had no brotherhood with me to abide by.

If they stayed downstairs, then maybe her wolf could relax a little and even enjoy the day.

My wolf was still on edge from Ayanna almost touching me. It had unsettled me too.

Sensing my unease, Josie stepped closer to my back and wrapped her arms around me.

My body shook and then relaxed instantly.

"Are you okay? You feel really tense," she said softly.

"I am now."

I turned in her arms and then reached up to caress her cheek before giving her a soft kiss. I wished she hadn't invited Karis and Damon to nap in our room. I needed to work off some of the frustrations I was feeling, and I had a pretty good idea that Josie naked beneath me would do just the trick.

Her eyes widened and her cheeks tinted as if she could somehow read my mind.

"I need to go check on Kian," I explained.

She nodded. "I'll just be hanging out here. Do what you need to do."

I grinned and waggled my eyebrows.

She playfully smacked me. "Later," she whispered.

I loved how the color flared in her cheeks. She had told me it was the curse of red hair. If that was the case, I was okay with it. It was cute and made me smile. Especially at times like this, because I loved knowing I affected her as much as she affected me.

It wasn't easy to leave her, but I forced myself too. I had obligations to my brothers too.

I walked down the hall to Kian's room and knocked on the door. There was no answer. I really hadn't expected there to be. I was just giving him a heads up that I was coming in.

I opened the door and let myself in. He was lying on his bed in just a pair of sweatpants and had his headphones on. Clearly Kian was in for the night, and I couldn't even blame him for it.

I shut the door behind me and pulled his desk chair next to the bed.

"Are they staying?" Kian asked as he took off his headphones and sat up in bed.

"No power, or so they said. Seeking shelter and all."

He groaned. "Did you actually believe that?"

I shrugged. "Chloe told me and she's often pretty straight with me. Plus, some of the other girls were complaining about it, so maybe. Theta showed up too. They have power, they're just bored."

He laughed. "I'm not surprised."

"They're all down in the basement if you want to come hang out. Most of the house went downstairs. There's only a few of us in the common room. Want to join us?"

"Nah, I'm good."

"You can't shut yourself off and ignore them forever."

He scoffed. "I don't expect you to understand."

"Oh you don't think I understand being looked at like I'm a piece of meat? For a while it was nice, fun even. But the second Ayanna moved to touch me, I wanted to rip out her throat."

He snorted. "I would have helped you bury the body."

"Hell yeah you would have. That's what brothers do."

He shook his head but smiled. "That's just your mating call."

"Maybe, but even before Josie arrived, I was over it. It gets old."

"It's more than that, man. Those are King Lockhardt's perfect kittens. He screams purity for the black cats, and yet, anyone from my pride is not worthy."

"What? That's insane. You're a pure bred, a black panther. Isn't that exactly what he wants to maintain?"

"Yup, and when I arrived that's exactly what he was hoping for. He wanted me to choose one of the girls here and mate her. He made that very clear."

"So what happened?"

"Another falling out with my father. Now those two fight like cats and dogs. It's getting bad. Lockhardt made an announcement basically disavowing my pride."

"After everything I've heard of the guy, I can't say I'm surprised."

"Well his order certainly hasn't stopped those girls. If anything, they're prowling even harder in defiance. I'm so sick of dealing with them. I honestly thought that moving into the doghouse would keep them far away, but I suppose after Jenna Lockhardt mated Chase Westin I should have known they'd all be prowling for dogs."

I groaned. "Between them and Theta, it's been a fulltime job this semester dealing with it all."

He snickered. "Chad really threw you to the wolves with that move."

I rolled my eyes. "Don't remind me."

"You're a great President here, Tyler."

"Thanks," I said quietly.

He stared at me. Kian was quieter than the others and sometimes I feared he thought he didn't fit in. We'd made him rush and pledge just like anyone else. As far as the rest of us were concerned, he was a brother, period. No one cared that Chad was a squirrel, and no one minded that Kian was a black panther. To us, they were simply brothers."

Sure, the doghouse was mostly comprised of wolves, but we'd had a variety of other canines over the years and a mixture of spirit animals that weren't canine at all. Kian wasn't even the first cat of Delta Omega Gamma.

I wasn't around when Matt Williams, a jaguar, was here. It was before my time, but we all knew the story and there was a picture of him that hung in the basement on a tribute wall.

When Jenna and Chase mated, a panther princess and essentially a wolf prince, all hell had broken loose. Jenna's father, King Lockhardt, had declared war against the wolves. It had been a bloody massacre. Chase was a brother of DOG and so the doghouse had bravely fought alongside him, supporting the wolves. That included Matt who had been deemed a traitor to the cats and died in the battle.

In the end a truce had been reached, but things between the cats and dogs were strained at best. Still Chase and Jenna couldn't be happier and I'd recently heard they were expecting their first kid. I didn't know them quite as well as some of the older brothers, but they had spent enough time around here for me to know enough.

I could honestly say that if I had been here, I would have stepped up and fought for them too, especially now that I truly understood the power of a mating bond. No one should ever come between that.

Kian was studying me. "Are you leaving?" he asked me.

"What? No."

"I heard Josie mention she needed to get back home. Where does that leave you?"

I huffed. "No clue. She's adamant about returning though. Has a new job starting on Monday. I'm proud of her for that, but the thought of her leaving really sucks."

"You're graduating in May, right? I mean like really graduating, not like these other assholes who can't seem to let this place go."

We both chuckled. "Yeah, I'm out of here. I don't feel like I need more than my bachelor's degree. At least not right now."

He nodded. "So three months isn't the end of the world."

"Then why does it feel like it is? I mean I'm dealing with it, and I know I have to graduate. I already have some inquiries in to my professors to see if I can do at least some of my classes remote so I can at least bounce back and forth and see her. We haven't exactly talked about that yet, but I'm trying to get things sorted as best as possible, because Josie leaving and me not seeing her for three months is not an option."

Kian nodded. "You're dealing with it all really well, Tyler."

"It doesn't feel that way. I mean that mess in the woods. Tim could have died out there and that's on me."

"It's not. There is nothing any of us wouldn't do for a brother or his mate. Plus, everything worked out okay. You can't carry that with you. You need to let it go."

"I know. Easier said than done."

He grinned. "I hear that. I can't even imagine myself. Panther true mates are very rare, probably because of the elitist snobs that say you can only mate a black panther. Keep the lineage pure and all that bullshit. I respect the hell out of Jenna for standing up for herself and following her heart. But when a panther finds her true mate as a dog, that's a sad testament to the state of the panthers right now."

I nodded. "I get it, but I can also say without a doubt, what spirit animal Josie carries has absolutely no bearing on how I feel about her. I wouldn't care what she was, just that she is mine."

"You're really lucky, man. I'm happy for you."

"If we can survive the next three months, then I'll be happy for me too."

"It's going to work out. You'll see."

"I sure hope you're right."

Josie

Chapter 20

I couldn't ever remember laughing so hard. I'd spent most of the afternoon hanging out with Amber and Ember. They were cracking me up with stories from the doghouse.

I'd seen Chad in his squirrel form. The things Ember said he'd done didn't even seem possible.

"How could he fight off a coyote? And a pack of tigers? That's insane."

"He has a psycho side to him and is absolutely fearless in squirrel form," Ember tried to explain.

I laughed so hard it hurt. I was holding my side, doubled over laughing when Tyler returned. He'd been gone for a while, but I wasn't really worried. The girls had all headed for the basement and he had gone down the hall. Not that it should have mattered. I trusted him, I just didn't really trust the girls. I'd seen more than one try to hit on him when they first arrived. It had set my wolf on edge, but I'd refused to let it get the best of me.

Ember had begun distracting me with stories.

I really liked her. She was absolutely nothing like the tabloids portrayed. The daughter of Hollywood's biggest diva and playboy father. Well the playboy part was recent. I had never read a negative thing about Martin Kenston until it had come out recently that he had a love child with another woman, a biological daughter when he and his wife, Alicia, couldn't have kids. It was common knowledge that Ember was adopted. I couldn't help but wonder if they even truly knew what she was.

"So how does that work?" I blurted out.

"What?" she asked.

"Well, you're adopted, right?"

"I am."

"And your parents are human?" I had never heard even the faintest rumor otherwise, so I assumed.

"They are," she said with a smile.

"You love them," I told her. It was written all over her face.

"They're the best parents in the entire world."

"But do they even know what you are?"

She pursed her lips and looked around. She didn't answer aloud, but she did nod.

"Wow. And you have a sister now? Is that true or just tabloid madness?"

"It's true. Dad didn't even know until about a month ago."

"Have you met her?"

"Yeah. Alaina's pretty great. We're still getting to know each other, but we talk often. She and her husband, Jake, are going to join us in Hawaii for spring break in a few weeks. It's still a little weird, but we're working through it as a family."

"That's really great. You're very lucky."

"Do you have siblings?"

I laughed. "No way. My parents never wanted kids. Mostly they still act like kids themselves."

She looked at me seriously and then frowned. "I'm sorry."

I shrugged. "It is what it is. Not everyone gets a glamorous fairytale ending."

"And yet, I hear you and Tyler were friends as kids and now reconnected after all these years only to find out you're true mates. That's the stuff real fairytales are made of, Josie. My life is just a carefully cultivated image. I actually grew up quite normal. Well, as normal as possible with your face splashed across every magazine in the world."

Tobi had joined us and snorted but nodded her head in agreement.

"The girls were telling me a little about what you were telling them. Is it true? The promise he made and all?"

I rolled my eyes and nodded.

"That is so sweet," Ember gushed. "I mean Tyler's always been one of the good ones. He was never as wild as the others."

"Yeah, more straight edged. Jackson says he's had his moments though."

"I don't know if I believe it," Jessie said as she and Marie joined me on the floor in front of the fire.

"One way to find out," Marie said with a grin.

"What do you mean?"

Amber groaned. "Marie's a witch. Careful Josie. She'll see right into your soul."

"You make it sound so ominous," Ember said with a laugh.

"Isn't it?" Amber challenged.

"It's hard on Marie to carry everyone else's burdens too," Jessie defended.

Marie shrugged. "I'm getting used to it. It's easier to compartmentalize things now."

She looked haunted though like she'd seen some terrible things in her life and made me shiver.

"I feel like we're in middle school and pulling out the Ouija board to try something scary," Tobi said.

The other girls burst out laughing.

"Yeah right. Is that something you and Landon did regularly in middle school?" Jess teased.

Tobi grinned. "I did try once. He was too chicken, but it was in a lot of scary movies and stuff. So seemed like something people did pretty regularly."

The girls cracked up again.

"I don't get it. Who's Landon?" I finally asked.

"My Alpha and best friend. He mated an honorary DOG last year."

My nose scrunched up. "As in she's not a wolf?"

"No, she's a wolf. I mean as in adopted into Delta Omega Gamma," Tobi said.

"Oh."

"Well, technically she was a Theta but she hung out here more than there, and I'm pretty sure it was only because the doghouse is all male," Jessie said.

"Except Kaitlyn. They all claim her as a DOG," Marie pointed out.

"Exactly," Tobi added, "and now she's my super cool Pack Mother and they are the cutest couple ever."

"Okay, so back to the Ouija board. What does that have to do with Marie?"

"It doesn't really. Just that her woo-woo sort of has that same thrill," Tobi explained.

"You're really a witch?" I asked Marie.

"I am. I used to be terrified of it, but now I embrace it. It's just a part of who I am. It's not like I can help it. I intern with Westin Force during the summer and that's really helped me to see it more as a gift and a way to help others instead of the curse I used to believe it to be."

"So how does it work?"

"She just looks into your eyes," Jessie explained.

"And right into your soul. No offense Marie, but she's a pretty private person. I don't think you want her poking around in your past, Josie," Amber warned.

"That's true," Marie confessed. "Sometimes if you're thinking about what it is you want verified then I can be in and out quickly, but if I go hunting for it, I see everything."

That haunted look was back in her eyes.

I gulped. "Everything?"

She nodded. "I never tell anyone. I mean for work that's a different story, but not when it's personal."

"She's not kidding either," Ember said. "No matter how many times we've tried to get her to tell us why Kaitlyn was so protected by the DOGs, she still won't spill it."

Tobi shrugged. "Landon knows and that's all that really matters. I can live without the details."

"Still not telling," Marie insisted. "You don't have to do this. It is true that sometimes I get drawn in, especially to darkness. That can be hard, so if you have demons in your past you don't want me to know about, then it's fine. Really. They just think it's fun to watch."

"Like a séance or the Ouija board," I said putting it all together.

"Exactly."

"You don't have to, Josie," Amber repeated. "It's okay to just have good memories of Tyler from your childhood without all the specific details."

"No, it's okay," I said. I had no idea why I was agreeing to this. I carried those memories close to my heart and always had. There was no doubt in my mind they were true. "Will I know everything you know?"

She nodded. "Yes. We're in this together."

"Okay. What can it hurt, right?"

I had an uneasy feeling about all she could learn about me, but I'd be leaving in a few days, and she had sworn she wouldn't tell anyone.

As I sat cross-legged before her and took her hands, I had a moment of regret, and then she looked into my eyes and instead of my wolf surging and recognizing it as a threat, her wolf stilled and the room around her faded into darkness.

Haunting memories flashed through my mind. The fears and tears. The lonely nights stuck in a van while they were gone. I couldn't hide any of it from her, and then suddenly there was a light. I ran towards it.

My heart warmed as I watched four-year-old Josie and Tyler on their first day of school. Sure it was only preschool, but it had been the first stable thing in my life and even as a young girl, I knew how momentous the moment had been.

"Hi. I'm Tyler Anthony Nigel Klein. I'm four and I lost my first tooth last night. See?"

The little girl giggled at the sight. "I'm Josie."

Scenes flashed through, resurrecting old memories. The good ones always included Tyler. Then it flickered to us at five. I was sitting out on the fire escape crying. Tyler poked his head out of his bedroom next door.

"What's wrong Jo-Jo?"

"Nothing," I said quickly.

"Aw, come on. You can tell me anything."

My stomach rumbled.

"Are you hungry?"

The younger version of me shook her head as a tear fell down my cheek. She swiped it away. "Go away, Ty. I'm fine."

"Are they gone again?"

"I said go away."

Much to the little girl's disappointment, he left.

Scared and alone she sat there with her knees tucked tightly to her chest. Her stomach rumbled again causing pains of emptiness. She couldn't remember when she had last ate but she already knew there was nothing but bad milk and moldy bread left in the house and she had no idea when her parents would return.

A few minutes later Tyler came back. He had a bowl of cereal and a big piece of cake in his arms as he crawled out onto the landing to sit beside her.

"Here. It's not much. I can't cook yet. I'm only five. But I'm gonna learn and I'm gonna take care of you, Jo-Jo. Mom says you can come to dinner tonight. I'll make some sandwiches for you to take home. And if you want, I can sneak over and stay with you tonight. I just have to wait for Richard to go to sleep or he'll tattle on me."

"Thanks, Ty."

The memory faded into others. A few included my parents and were still good memories, like the day they took us to Central Park to play in the snow.

Some included Tyler's family. His mother had always been exactly the way a mother should be as far as I was concerned. A scene played out of her letting me and Tyler help make and decorate Christmas cookies. I didn't remember the moment. I couldn't remember any Christmas celebrations in my life. Aunt Courtney always worked Christmas Eve at the diner where she worked third shift. We never even bothered to put up a tree or exchange presents.

A new scene surfaced and I started to breathe heavy with emotions.

"I'm leaving, Ty. We're moving."

"But they don't even want you. Stay here with me and I'll take care of you."

"I can't. I'm just a kid."

"We could talk to the Alpha."

"He'll never listen. Besides, they've already loaded up the van. There's nothing I can do."

"They can't just take you away from me. You're my best friend, Jo-Jo."

The little girl hugged him. “I love you, Tyler. I’ll never forget you.”

“Being a kid sucks. When I grow up and get my wolf, I’m gonna find you and make you my mate. I’ll always take care of you. I promise. I love you, Josie.”

Everything faded back to black and slowly the room came back into view. Marie looked shaken and tears streaked her cheeks. She wrapped her arms around me and hugged me tightly.

“So did the promise happen?” Tobi asked.

“Oh my gosh, yes. It was heartbreakingly beautiful. That promise he made to you, and now that the two of you have found each other again, girl, that’s the shit true fairytales are made of,” Marie gushed.

I didn’t want to be a downer, so I smiled and let them enjoy the moment, but the truth was, I hadn’t gotten my fairytale ending because Tyler had never come for me.

Tyler

Chapter 21

I could hear the girls talking as I walked down the hall. Marie was gushing over some promise and telling everyone it was true.

"I mean Tyler's always been a great guy, but that was the sweetest thing I've ever witnessed," Marie gushed. "Who knew even as a kid he was such a romantic."

I groaned, trying to think what on *Earth* Josie could have divulged about me. We were so young. I only had pieces of memories from that time in my life.

I walked in and cleared my throat. "Ladies. Hope I'm not interrupting anything."

"No, nothing," Tobi said. She was a terrible liar.

"Josie, are you hungry? I was going to make us some food."

Marie sighed and grabbed her hand. "He really did follow through on that one."

Josie shot her a look and then stood up. "Want some help?"

"Sure."

She followed me into the kitchen.

"What was that all about?" I asked her.

"Nothing," she said a little too quickly.

It made me feel good to feed Josie and know she wasn't hungry. I didn't really understand why. I assumed it was just a need to care for her, now heightened by the mating call, but I had a feeling the girls were poking fun at me for it.

Anytime I heard her stomach growl it caused me physical pain and an obsessive need to feed her. Yet anytime I set foot in the kitchen, my brothers got excited and demanded I cook for everyone. It was a catch twenty-two.

"Are we feeding everyone?"

"No," I said. I'd wasted enough time cooking for those fools "Is beef stew, okay?" I asked her.

"Sounds delicious."

I took two containers out of the freezer and tossed them into the microwave. It was the fastest thing I could think of.

"I'd make you some fresh bread to go with it, but if I start baking, they'll smell it and then we'll be hours in this kitchen tonight."

She laughed. "I really don't mind either way."

When the soup was done, I grabbed two spoons and the bowls and headed for the bedroom.

Josie wanted to knock, so I juggled both containers and opened the door myself.

Damon and Karis were awake and changing the sheets on the bed.

"You didn't have to do that," Josie insisted.

"Please, it's the least we can do. Thank you for loaning us your bed for a few hours. I really needed some decent sleep," Karis said.

I quickly caught them up on what was going on in the house and warned them about both the Theta and Panther houses crashing here.

"How's Kian handling them being here?" Damon asked, sounding sincerely concerned.

"Hiding in his room as usual."

"I'll check on him."

"I already did, but I'd still appreciate it if you would. I know his kind tends to be loaners to begin with, but I still worry about him."

"Wouldn't be shit for a leader if you didn't," Damon teased.

"Wait, are you saying I'm *not* shit for a leader?"

He shrugged. "You let me sleep in your bed. I'm feeling nicer than usual."

I scrunched up my nose, looked at the bed then back to him as he wrapped an arm around his mate.

"Dammit. You did it in my bed?"

Karis's face flushed as she elbowed him in the gut.

"Who do I have to thank for the dampener in here?"

I shook my head and chuckled. "Jackson."

Karis sniffed the air. "Wait, did you make beef stew again?"

"No," I said.

Damon sniffed. "That's definitely your beef stew. You told us there wasn't anymore."

"Because I froze the leftovers," I finally blurted out.

"So there is more?" Karis demanded.

I gave an exaggerated sigh. "It's in the freezer, just warm it up," I conceded.

Karis actually squealed in delight and then kissed my cheek.

Josie growled which made me grin.

"Come on, I'm starving," she said, dragging Damon from the room.

I followed them and locked the door behind them.

"Eat up," I told Josie.

She gave me a funny look. "When did you learn to cook so well?"

I shrugged. "Don't know. Mom says I was pretty young when I started begging for lessons. So in a way, it was just something I always enjoyed."

Tears coated her eyes and I started to panic.

"Just what exactly were you guys doing when I walked in?"

"It was nothing," she said, brushing me off once more.

She took a small bite knowing the stew would be hot. Then she moaned in appreciation and gave me a thumbs up.

"So what's that promise Marie was gushing over?"

Josie started choking. She coughed and started turning red in the face. I couldn't tell if it was her usual embarrassment or if she simply couldn't breathe.

I tried to stay calm and passed her a bottle of water.

She sputtered a bit more before finding her breath again. She didn't answer my question though. Instead, she shoved in another mouthful of stew.

I wasn't sure if I should press the issue or let it drop. In the end, I backed off. Whatever fairytale promise the girls had been gushing over would have to wait. Besides, real life with my one true mate was proving to be far better than any fairytale ever could be.

We sat quietly eating. It always amazed me how much pleasure just feeding my girl brought me. It was crazy, but I was grateful for all that time in the kitchen growing up learning my mother's best recipes and later creating my own.

"This is really delicious, Ty," she said.

I couldn't remember her calling me that, at least not since she'd shown up here a few days ago, and back in my life.

Had it really only been a few days?

It felt like a lifetime. Between early memories and now, the gaping hole in between just seemed empty.

How bad was it going to be when she left?

I pushed that thought aside knowing the fear of it would consume me.

Instead, I smiled. "I'm glad you like it, Jo-Jo."

She groaned and shook her head, but she smiled. The last time I'd nearly used the old nickname, she'd glared and warned me to back off. I wondered what had changed, but I didn't ask.

The music kicked on from the basement, and since my room was on the first floor, there was no way we could hide from it. Those with bedrooms on the second floor had a mildly better buffer, though with our accelerated wolf hearing, it wasn't much of an improvement.

"Sorry," I said with a groan. "One of the downfalls of living in a fraternity house. We do try to limit the number of parties we have each month, or at least rotate around between the other houses."

Josie shrugged. "It sounds like fun."

I gave her a weird look. "Do you want to head down and join in?"

She bit her lip drawing my full attention to them. When her tongue lashed out and wet them, I had to kiss her.

I closed that gap between us in record time pulling her into my arms and kissing her like my life depended on it.

My hands found the curve of her ass and gently lifted her as she wrapped her legs around my waist. I wasn't even sure exactly how I managed to get us naked, but it wasn't long before I had her up against the door thrusting into her with an unexplained madness.

My canines kept elongating, demanding I claim her, but I pushed it off and devoured her in every other way. It was quick and frenzied but I had never felt so alive. I was completely connected to her. There was a thrill and fear in that realization.

Josie held my heart in her hands, and it was hers to cherish or destroy.

A rumble ran through me as I found my release. Her moan had the edge of a scream to it as she held on to me for dear life and fell limp in my arms.

I just held her there braced against my bedroom door breathing in her space and cherishing every second that she was mine, because a small part of me was just waiting for her to run away again and this time, I didn't know if I could survive it.

"I'm sorry," I finally said, still a little breathless.

She pulled back to look at me. Her eyes were still just a little hazed over from our frantic love making.

"For what?"

"I don't know what came over me," I confessed. "I just knew I had to have you."

A slow smile crossed her face. "That's not something you ever have to apologize for Tyler."

I kissed her again, slower this time.

"Do you still want to go down to the party?"

She bit her lip again and I sucked in a sharp breath.

She pursed them instead and giggled softly.

"I think it will be fun. I've never really been to a party before."

I looked at her like she was crazy.

"Never?"

She shook her head, and I knew she was telling the truth by the color across her cheeks.

"Not even prom?"

She frowned and then shook her head again.

"Were all the guys in your school blind idiots?"

That made her laugh, but I was damn serious. Josie was beautiful and she was sultry as hell. I was struggling just to keep my hands off of her. How had no one ever asked her to prom or tried to snag her before now?

My wolf growled in my head and I knew I should be rejoicing in that fact, but at the same time it made me sad for her.

"Get dressed," I said, making the decision for us. "We're going dancing."

She laughed as I set her down to the floor loving the feel of her smooth skin melded against mine.

"You dance?"

"Of course I dance. You don't?"

She looked a little terrified. "Not in front of people."

She was adorable when she was flustered, and I adored her.

"Just follow my lead because I'm not letting you out of my arms down there. I'm holding it together okay with my brothers around. They know to keep their distance, but I can't promise the girls will be so nice about it."

She snorted. "Are you worried about them for me or you?"

I grinned. "I mean a few of them could swing either way. I don't know how my wolf will deal with one of them hitting on you."

She giggled. "Tyler, I'm serious."

But so was I.

"Just stay by my side and I'm sure we'll be fine."

"And if things go badly? I mean, I didn't exactly like the way one of them looked at you when they arrived." Her face was nearly the same color as her hair and I knew it had been hard for her to admit that to me.

"If things go bad, then I'm dragging you up here and marking you once again as mine."

She gasped and reached for her neck. There was a hint of fear in her eyes.

"I didn't mean it like that. I mean, I do want that, but only when you're as sure as I am."

The truth of that hurt. I knew I wanted to spend the rest of my life with Josie by my side, but I wasn't certain that's what she wanted.

"Tyler, I…"

I silenced her with a kiss. "It's okay. We'll talk about all of that later. Parties are supposed to be light and fun. No heavy stuff."

She sighed but conceded. "What should I wear?"

"I'm just going in jeans and a button down shirt."

She held up several different tops to show me finally settling on a pretty flowered crop top. It showed off enough skin for my personal pleasure, but also just enough to put my wolf on high alert the second we stepped out of the room and made our way down to the party in the basement.

Josie

Chapter 22

My body was still buzzing. Whatever had come over Tyler to make him take me so quickly right against the door like that had sparked a new thrill of desire within me. There was just something so powerful and fulfilling about a man losing control like that, while somehow managing to still remain fully in control.

It had made my head spin and left a perma-grin on my face.

I was a little nervous about heading down to the party. Just another one of many firsts Tyler had showed me in our time together.

If it had been anyone else suggesting it, I would have chickened out and turned it down, maybe even fake a headache, or claim to be too tired.

But it had been him, and I wanted this. I wanted to experience everything with Tyler.

He took my hand as we reached the bottom.

I took a look around surprised by how nice it looked. Maybe not like super nice, but it was pretty much everything I imagined a fraternity house would look like. It was in sharp contrast to upstairs where everything was much homier than I would have expected.

Tyler gave my hand a squeeze of encouragement and headed for the dance floor.

My stomach knotted up. I hadn't lied when I told him I had never been to a party, and had never danced in front of people before. The music was thumping and it was hard not to be intimidated by some of the girls dancing sexy in the center of the room.

Some of the guys stood around with beers just watching. Others were joining in. With two sororities showing up it was obvious that there were more females than males.

It took a bit before people started to notice our arrival, or rather Tyler's arrival.

Two girls danced over towards us and tried to pull him away from me to drag him out with them. I let out a low growl of warning.

"I'm good," Tyler told them but one of them wasn't taking no for an answer. "I said, I'm good." He was a little more assertive this time.

The girl looked me over and rolled her eyes. "Your loss."

She sauntered off and I moved closer to Tyler.

He grinned as he let go of my hand and wrapped a possessive arm around me.

Holden and Marie took control of the situation and ran around warning people to back off from the two of us. I caught enough of their whispers to understand they were making it clear that Tyler and I weren't stable due to mating.

I groaned and buried my face into his chest.

This wasn't a good idea.

He put his hands on my hips and started to move. It didn't even register what he was doing until I suddenly realized we were dancing.

My body was molded against his, swaying along as if we were one body. It felt like the most natural thing in the world. His hands roamed up the side of my body and positioned my arms on his shoulders.

I looked up and wasn't prepared for the heat I saw in his deep blue eyes.

He kissed me and I realized that in his own way he was officially claiming me. Of course, his brothers and their mates already knew about us, but I didn't think he was leaving anything just to rumors where the girls were concerned.

I snuck a peek around the room and realized people were now watching us. My cheeks started to burn.

"Josie, eyes up here. Just look at me. No one else in this room matters."

I did as he said and was lost in his eyes. The rest of the room faded away until it felt like it was just the two of us. I followed his lead and moved when he moved. I didn't feel silly or even self-conscious. It was sexy and hot.

My body was recharged and so was his. I could practically hear the low drum of electricity pulsing between us, and I ached for him. It was only made worse by the most incredible smell surrounding us. It made my mouth water and my desire spike even higher.

It felt as though I was floating on a cloud high in the sky. All I saw was Tyler. The world could burn around us, and I wouldn't have noticed.

I had no idea how long we'd been dancing like that completely absorbed in each other, but when the music stopped, the magical spell took a hit.

I looked around surprised to find we really were all alone.

"Where'd everyone go?"

Tyler looked around clearly as confused as I felt.

"I don't know. I guess we should check on them."

I nodded.

He took my hand and we walked back upstairs.

The common room was cram packed with people everywhere.

"What's going on?" Tyler asked Damon.

Damon smirked. "You sort of got lost in your mate."

I blushed furiously and grabbed hold of Tyler's arm.

"And you stunk up the whole basement," Jamie announced. "Dude it was bad."

Jackson laughed. "My little bro's right. You were scenting."

"I'd already taken the hint and backed off. You didn't have to scent the whole room," the girl that had been flirting with him said.

"Did I really do that?" he asked. Then he turned to look at me. "Did you smell it?"

I shook my head. "I thought it smelled good down there."

Karis burst out laughing. "When you clear a room and only your mate thinks it smells nice, then you are absolutely scenting, Tyler."

He sighed. "Sorry guys. I didn't know."

"Want me to check it now?" Denny asked.

"Yeah, sure," Chad said with a snicker as the kid ran downstairs, happy to help out.

And then he ran right back up. "Nope, still stinks."

Everyone started laughing.

I expected Tyler to be embarrassed, but instead he just shrugged and then kissed me in front of everyone.

There were whoops and cheers all around.

I smiled against his lips.

"Don't get him started again," Asher warned.

It would take half an hour longer before one of the sacrificial pledges would declare it safe to return to the basement.

"Do you want to dance some more. Try it again?" Tyler asked me.

"No!" Damon and Chad yelled in unison.

"Let the kids enjoy the rest of the evening," Jackson said. He and Tobi were already battling it out on the Xbox.

With just Chad, Jackson, and Damon remaining along with their mates, Tyler and I took a seat on one of the couches.

"I really think everyone was exaggerating," I muttered, still a little embarrassed by the fact that I had been so wrapped up in Tyler that I didn't even notice everyone leaving.

"He's your mate, Josie. It's supposed to smell great to you," Karis explained.

"It's really more of a wolf thing, but even I could smell it," Ember admitted.

"He can't help it," Tobi insisted before jumping up and throwing her hands in the air. "In your face, Jackson. Admit defeat now!"

"Ignore them," Karis said. "They're both extremely competitive."

"Is that the new version of Chaos?" I asked.

"Do you game?" Tyler asked me.

"Not really. I watch Amber's little brother pretty regularly though and he's obsessed with the game. His birthday's coming up and I've been waiting for it to release hoping to surprise him, but I'm not holding my breath either. That's like the hottest game of the year."

Jackson grinned and reached into a bag at his feet. He pulled out a disk that also had a download code on it and tossed it to me.

My eyes widened. "Are you serious? This is the game? But it doesn't release for another two weeks."

Jackson shrugged. "I know a guy."

Tobi snorted. "He wrote the program, Josie. It's what he does. So I literally just beat him at his own game."

Everyone laughed as Jackson groaned.

"Are you messing with me?" I asked not sure if I believed them or not.

"He's serious," Tyler said. "We get all the latest and greatest games thanks to him."

"That's really cool."

I felt a little lacking in their presence. Ember and Chad were practically Hollywood legends. Karis and Damon would some day run their own Pack. Now, Jackson was practically a gaming legend. I was way out of my league with these people.

I was just a nurse, nothing special really.

No sooner had I thought that there came a scream from downstairs. The guys took off quickly to see what was happening.

A few minutes later they returned, carrying Hudson with Holden right on their heels.

"What the hell happened?" Tyler demanded.

"I don't know. He was just dancing, and I think he slipped or something. Anyway, he went one way, and his foot went the other," Holden explained.

"I think it's broke," Hudson said between gritted teeth.

"Broke?" Holden yelled. "It can't be broke. The NFL is scouting him. A broken ankle could end his career before it even begins. Tyler you have to get him help."

"I can take him over to the clinic on the snowmobile, but there's no guarantee that anyone will even be there in this weather," Damon said.

"There's no guarantee that they even have power over there," Jackson pointed out.

My training kicked into gear.

"Move out of the way," I said, pushing my way through to Hudson. "Tyler scoot him up further on the couch. I don't want his leg elevated, I need it flat."

Tyler didn't stop to ask questions. He just did as I asked.

People started coming back upstairs to check on him.

"Get them out of here," I insisted but it wasn't helping any. I huffed in frustration. "Just take him to his room and keep everyone out," I shouted, loud enough this time for people to take notice.

Damon and Jackson carefully picked him up again as Hudson cried out in pain. They got him to a room on the first floor just a few doors down from Tyler's.

Kian stepped out of his room curious about the commotion.

"What happened?" he asked.

"Looks like Hudson broke his ankle," Tyler said.

"Shit! I can assist."

"Josie?" Tyler asked me.

"Do you have any medical experience I asked?"

"I'm a volunteer paramedic back home."

"Perfect. You come with me. Tyler, keep the rest of them out."

"I'm not leaving him," Holden insisted.

I sighed. "Fine. Come on. I need to set it quickly."

"Do you know how to do that?" Kian asked.

"Piece of cake," I said with a wink. The natural high of an emergency was starting to kick in and my focus was razor sharp.

Damon and Jackson left to assist Chad with keeping everyone at bay.

Tyler stood guard at the door.

Holden paced on his side of the room, never a good sign for a wolf shifter.

"We have to move quickly and there is no time for drugs here, Hudson. Do you hear me? If I don't set this before your wolf tries to heal you, then you could have severe long term problems with it."

"Whatever you can do to help. Just do it. I can take it."

But when I went to just move his pants, Hudson cried out in pain and jerked his leg from me.

"You might have to hold him down," I told Kian.

"I can do that."

"Or…" I considered my options. "Holden, can you please go and get Marie. I need her help." As soon as he left, I turned back to Kian. "Restrain him. I don't know how long Holden will be.

I waited for Kian to secure him before starting my evaluation. It was bad but felt like a pretty clean break. Without an x-ray machine I couldn't be absolutely certain, but I had certainly seen worse.

Before I had started to attempt at setting the break, Holden returned with Marie.

I turned to her. "Can you do that mind thing on Hudson? Maybe take him to a happy place? Can you even do that? If I wait for pain meds to kick in, he'll risk permanent damage to this ankle, but he's in so much pain."

"Do what you have to do. I'll take care of his pain."

Marie sat down on the edge of the bed and took Hudson's hand. Sweat had broken out across his brow. As soon as she looked into his eyes, his thrashing body stilled.

"Wow," Kian said.

"Yeah, wow."

"What do we need to do, boss?"

"Keep holding that leg down just in case while I try to manipulate everything back into place."

"Would it be better if he shifted?"

"No. He could lose serious mobility in it if it heals wrong."

I concentrated hard, remembering my training and feeling my way through. I had gone through a human training program to study, but I had also worked closely with the Pack physician back home.

I could hear Simon now. "Shifters are different, Josie. We heal much faster so you have to stay calm and work quickly. There won't always be time or availability for machines when we want them. Close your eyes and feel your way through."

I sucked in a deep breath and then slowly released it allowing myself to calm as I closed my eyes and remembered the lessons Simon had taught me.

Identifying the swelling points was my first step. Feeling for the break. As gently as possible I moved things around working to realign his ankle.

Time stood still, or maybe it didn't. I had no real measure of it.

I was slightly aware of the way Kian was watching my every move. I heard the pop realizing there was some dislocation factored in. With that set I pulled and tugged until I was at last satisfied that everything was back the way it should be.

I opened my eyes. Kian was staring at me with a look of wonder.

"Do you have any bandages or casting molds that we can secure this with?"

"Actually, I do. I have my med kit in my room. There should be everything you need."

"Great."

Kian left the room to retrieve it. I could hear people in the hallway asking questions and demanding to know how he was doing.

"Back off and let them work," Tyler told them.

Once Kian was back, he carefully wrapped Hudson's ankle with some gauze. Next, he handed me two pieces of casting that was already wet. I carefully shaped them to each side of his ankle and then Kian finished it off by securing them with an ace bandage while I held things in place.

"Great job," I told him, happy with the results. It wasn't half bad for an emergency job in the middle of a snowstorm.

"You were wonderful," Kian said.

I blushed at his compliment. "It was nothing."

"Is he going to be okay?" Holden asked.

I smiled reassuringly. "If he behaves and stays off of it for a few days, then he should be perfectly fine. If there's a trainer or physical therapist on campus, they might want to look at him, but I want a slow healing for two to three days."

"If he shifts too soon the bones could fuse together wrong," Kian explained.

"Exactly."

"Okay. He'll do whatever you tell him to, Josie. I'll make sure of it."

Holden crossed the room and threw his arms around my neck. "Thank you."

"Marie, you can let him go now."

I wasn't certain she heard me at first, but then slowly she came out of the trance she had him in.

Hudson winced, but quickly admitted the pain was tolerable.

Kian was already shoving a combination of Tylenol and Ibuprofen down his throat.

"Holden, I need his foot elevated to help with swelling."

"You got it, Josie."

He retrieved two pillows to carefully prop Hudson's leg up.

"I'm okay. I'm okay," Hudson repeated, a sure sign he was suffering just a bit of shock from the experience.

"You're going to be fine, Hudson."

When I rose from the bed, Marie hugged me.

"Thank you," she whispered.

"Thank you. You made my job pretty easy."

"You guys make a great team," Kian said.

I reached out and squeezed his hand. "The three of us made a great team."

The adrenaline of the moment was fading quickly and I knew there was nothing else I could do. Kian followed up with some basic instructions and I knew my patient was going to be in good hands under Holden and Marie's close supervision.

I stepped outside to find Tyler still standing in the hallway.

"How is he?"

I smiled. "He's going to be fine."

Cheers rang out from down the hall. With a bunch of wolves in the house I wasn't at all surprised they had heard me.

"Are you okay?" Tyler asked me.

I nodded. "Just a normal day's work."

"You are amazing. I don't know what we would have done if you hadn't been here and stepped up like that."

I stepped into his embrace knowing I was about to be kissed.

Karis and Damon walked down the hall and she didn't even care that Tyler and I were having a moment. She wrapped her arms around the two of us and hugged us tight.

Tyler

Chapter 23

One day at a time. That was what we had agreed to, and it was working in my favor.

The next day, the sun came out and warmed up enough to melt all of the snow. It caused flooding in several buildings around campus and ensured school was cancelled for the remainder of the week.

By the time Friday arrived Josie still hadn't said a word about leaving and I sure as hell wasn't going to bring it up.

We'd settled into a nice routine and I couldn't imagine not waking up next to her every single day. My bed was around a combination of both our scents despite the fact that we hadn't sealed our bond yet. Each time we were intimate that became harder for me to put off.

My wolf was insistent and becoming more aggressive towards others the longer I took to sink my teeth into her skin just at the base of the slender column of her neck.

I stared down at her sleeping form beside me as I held her close and my canines started to appear just thinking about it.

I forced them back and kissed her there instead as she stretched.

Groggily she looked up at me. "Good morning."

I kissed her, needing her like a drug addict needed a hit.

"Mine," I growled.

She giggled and pushed me back.

"We should talk first."

I groaned. "My plans for you are far more enjoyable."

"Tyler," she scolded.

"Fine. What do you want to talk about?"

She took a deep breath and tears pricked her eyes, setting my wolf on high alert.

"I booked my flight last night. I leave tomorrow afternoon. It will give me a day to regroup before I start my new job."

My jaw dropped and then I forced it closed. I didn't need to react to this. She had been completely honest with me, and I knew it was coming. I couldn't lash out and blame her for it no matter how miserable the idea made me.

I had only heard back from two of five professors. Both denied my request for remote classes due to in person labs I was required to attend. They did say they would allow me to work ahead though and possibly extend my upcoming spring break by a week or two without penalty due to the circumstances.

Still, that was at least three weeks away. How was I going to survive without Josie for three weeks?

The only thing I knew without a doubt was that I had to stand by her through better or worse. I would support her decision no matter how much it hurt me.

I took a deep breath and let it out. "Okay."

"Okay?"

"Okay."

"But…"

"Josie, you've made it clear how important this new job is to you. You've been nothing but honest about it. I've tried to work things out so I can go with you, but it's not working." In a way I felt like a failure, like I'd somehow let her down. "I need to stay here and finish my degree."

Tears spilled from her big blue eyes as she nodded.

I cradled her close to me.

"I know it's not going to be easy, but we're going to get through this. I promise."

"Please don't promise. I can't handle it if you find you can't or decide you don't want to follow through with it."

"Look at me sweetheart, there is nothing in this world that will ever make me want anything more than you."

"You say that now, but when I'm gone, you'll go back to your life and forget me… again."

She said that final word so softly I almost missed it. The sadness in her voice told me I had let her down already, or maybe before, but for the life of me, I couldn't figure it out.

I remembered talk of a promise amongst the girls. Had I promised her something when we were little and failed to follow through with it?

"I've already let you down. I don't know how to fix this. Tell me how."

She sniffed and wiped at her eyes. "You haven't let me down, Tyler."

"But I did."

"What?"

"I overheard some of what you and the girls were talking about a few days ago. Something about a promise. Did I make you a promise before?"

She stared at me and frantically shook her head, but I knew she was lying.

I wasn't prepared for the stabbing pain that shot through my heart.

A promise?

When I grow up and get my wolf, I'm gonna find you and make you my mate. I'll always take care of you. I promise. I love you, Josie.

The memory was suddenly so vivid in my mind that I couldn't believe it was the first time I was remembering it.

"Mine," I whispered. "I love you, Josie."

She sobbed and buried her face in my shirt.

"I did let you down. I didn't come for you when my wolf came in. I don't even know how I would have ever found you after all those years."

I stroked her back.

"I should have come for you."

"Stop," she said. "It was a stupid childhood promise."

I could see in her eyes that she was lying once more.

"It wasn't to you."

She shrugged. "I was stupid, and I grew up and stopped believing in fairytales a long time ago, Tyler."

"Then what do you call this?"

"What do you mean?"

"I made a promise to you that when I grew up and my wolf came in that I was going to find you and make you mine. I might have been a little late, Josie, but I'm here and I'm yours. Just say the word and I will proudly mark you as mine."

Her breath caught as she stared up at me. Her eyes watered again but I didn't think they were sad tears this time.

"Karis says I shouldn't leave before we seal our bond, that it will be too hard on you and cause physical pain. Is that true?"

I shrugged. "It's possible, but I can handle it if you aren't ready for that, Josie."

She chewed on her bottom lip and considered the options.

I tipped her chin up to look at me.

"I'm not going to let you down ever again, sweetheart. You are mine. Period. I don't know how else to tell you that or prove it to you without sealing our bond."

"But what happens when I'm back in Virginia and you're here?"

I knew that was bothering her. It was bothering me too.

"I'll miss you like crazy. I will wake up in the middle of the night reaching for you. I will probably call enough to drive you insane, and I will definitely need daily video calls at a minimum. If possible, I will fly up on the weekends, but I understand that you could be working weekends too. Don't be surprised if I show up anyway just to hold you in my arms while you sleep or bring you food on your break to make sure you're getting enough to eat."

She hiccupped and nodded as the tears flowed freely now, but there was a smile on her face.

"You do like to feed me."

I nodded. "I do. It makes me feel good to care for you. My point is, I have three months left here, Josie. Just three. It feels like an eternity right now considering facing them without you, but I know in the big picture of our life together, it's only going to be a blip. I just have to remind myself constantly that I am doing this for you, for us, and for our future."

"But then what? You'll expect me to go back to New York with you, and I don't know if I can handle that."

"I'll talk to your Alpha, Josie."

She gave me a confused look and I chuckled.

"I don't want to go back to New York. I had already made my mind up on that before you. I always thought I would, but I've never had so much space and freedom before coming here. I don't think I can give that up for life in a busy city again."

"We have lots of Pack land to run on," she said.

"I know. I've already asked around some. If your Alpha will have me, I am fine with following you there. I've only spoken with him briefly, but I have a feeling he'll be okay with it."

"You talked to Daniel?"

"Well, yeah. I wanted to introduce myself and make sure it was going to be okay to visit you once you're back in his territory."

"You really did that?"

"Of course. I will take care of you, Josie. And I do love you."

I caressed her cheek while she cried some more, but there was a light in her eyes and I could feel her happiness through our bond.

"You really want me?"

"More than anything, sweetheart. You can still choose not to accept me, but for me, you're it. I will never accept another."

She kissed me hard on the lips. I could taste her salty tears and I wanted to kiss away every last one.

Pulling back suddenly she gave me an odd look. "Tyler?"

"Yeah?"

"Be honest with me."

"Always."

"Do you think it will make things better or worse if we were to seal our bond before I go?"

"I really don't know, Josie. From what I've seen and heard, things get easier after a bond is sealed, but being apart? I don't think anything will make that easier."

"I'm so sorry, Tyler."

"No, don't. We're going to get through this and someday probably look back and laugh."

"I'm not sure I believe that."

I shrugged and grinned. "You never know. The only thing I do know is you are mine and the next few months will suck, but when it's over, I'll be able to take care of you and support us. The rest, we have a lifetime ahead of us to figure it all out."

She worried her lip again.

"I don't know if it will help any to be bonded, but I think it would help me believe you'll come back to me."

My heart felt light, and I could breathe a little easier.

I could already feel my teeth elongating with my wolf's glee and anticipation. He didn't want to wait a second longer, and neither did I.

I smiled brightly to show them to Josie.

Her eyes widened.

"Now?"

I shrugged. "I told you, I'm ready when you are," I told her with a slight lisp from my oversized teeth.

"I've loved you since I was four years old. Tyler, for me, there's never been another, and there never will be."

She kissed me and then leaned back and smiled to show me her canines too.

Josie

Chapter 24

We were really doing this. I had butterflies in my stomach equal parts excitement and nerves. I had no idea what to expect.

"You're shaking."

"Sorry. Just nervous."

"Talk to me, Josie. What are you scared of?"

"I'm not afraid. I'm just nervous because I have no idea what to expect."

"Neither do I," Tyler admitted.

We both laughed. It helped to cut through the tension knowing we were in this together.

He kissed me. It heated quickly as my lips parted on a sigh. Tongue and teeth clashed in a sudden desperation. It was odd because I could feel the sharp points of his canines. They should have terrified me, but instead it brought on a sort of excitement.

We were both naked already, a sleeping habit we had formed somewhere along the way.

His hands skimmed down my body sending a shiver through me.

I knew him, every inch of him, and yet this time something felt different, almost like the first time. I knew it was because this moment was that important. We would both remember it as clearly as our first time making love, maybe even more so.

"You're sure about this?" he asked in a deep husky voice that told me he was already turned on, hot, and ready to take me to places only he and I existed.

I stared into his dark blue eyes and the peace I felt was all the confirmation I needed.

"I'm ready."

Still, he didn't rush it. He kissed me again down the column of my neck to stop and stare as if he were picking out the perfect spot to mark me as his.

My breathing increased in anticipation and need deep within me, I ached for him.

He seemed to make up his mind as he sucked on one particularly sensitive spot, but he didn't sink his teeth into me. Instead, he continued his path of torture to give full attention to my breasts as he sucked one pert nipple into his mouth.

My hands fisted in his hair as I held him there, lavishing in the pleasure he was causing to pool between my legs. As if sensing my need, he moved to the other breast while his hand toyed with me, heightening my need for him.

The orgasm came so quickly it surprised me. I gasped and my hips bucked against his hand.

He sat back and looked at me with such a fierceness in his eyes.

"Mine," he growled and just as my body began to splinter into a million pieces, he lowered his head and bit my neck.

I froze in shock and then completely let go.

I cried out in sheer bliss as I sunk my teeth into him marking him as mine and sealing a bond that could never be broken.

For one perfect moment we stilled just like that.

I didn't think anything could possibly feel better than that single moment of absolute connection, but then he settled over me and plunged inside in one swift thrust.

Completely bonded in heart, body, and soul.

I couldn't stay still for long. I was still so sensitive and could feel the pressure building as I moved, seeking relief. I had never needed that more than I did now.

I could taste his sweet blood in my mouth, and it made me feel like I was flying high. I was invincible and filled with unwavering need for Tyler.

A sort of frenzy began and I knew he was right there with me as we groped and groaned, touched and loved, bringing each other to the point of ecstasy like never before.

I was struggling to catch my breath, but I wasn't ready to let go.

It was wild and freeing, better than anything I could have ever prepared myself for.

We climaxed together still stuck in that perfect blissful bubble.

He retracted his teeth first and licked at the spot of blood left there. I followed his lead feeling satiated and happier than ever before—complete. I felt whole for the first time in my life.

He stared down at me in complete awe. The light in his eyes told me he was happy, but if there had been any doubt it was laid to rest by the fact that I could vividly feel his happiness.

He kissed my lips sweetly.

"Officially mine."

I sighed, feeling more content than ever.

We'd done it. We had sealed our bond. He was truly mine. This time when I left it would only be a momentary parting because he would always belong by my side.

The tears sprang up suddenly.

I had been alone for so long. I'd never really had someone to call my own. My parents certainly hadn't fulfilled that roll. I'd had no siblings or even cousins that I was aware of. And while Aunt Courtney had tried to fill just a bit of that emptiness, it just wasn't really in her. She simply wasn't the maternal type and a part of me feared I never would be either.

"Shh. Don't cry. I'm so sorry, Josie."

"Sorry? What?"

"You're obviously upset about our bonding."

I rolled my eyes and shook my head. "Close your eyes and feel my emotions, Tyler."

He did and grinned. "Happy?"

"So happy!"

I kissed him sweetly.

"Just overwhelmed with emotions."

He rolled to his side and pulled me partially on top of him.

"Me too," he confessed.

"When I leave, I really won't lose you now?" I asked. I needed to know the answer to that.

"We're bonded now, Josie. You can't get rid of me even if you wanted to."

I gave him another quick kiss.

"Thank God."

He frowned. "Were you really worried about that?"

I shrugged. "Maybe a little."

"I'm your mate. You're stuck with me for better or worse. Maybe the next three months will be for worse, but we're going to get through it. I'm not kidding when I said I would need to obsessively talk to you and see you through video chats every single day. If it weren't for the fact that I'm in my last semester with only a few months until graduation, then I would just drop out and finish up next year at a school near you."

"You can't do that, Tyler. You're so close to graduation."

"I know," he said, sounding a little sad. "And I keep telling myself it'll pay off for us in the future to stick it out. Still, I hate this. I'm going to miss you like crazy."

"I'm going to miss you too."

I was wavering on my decision to leave. Was this job really worth being apart from him? I had worked so hard for it and I knew it was the responsible thing to do. It didn't feel like the right thing at that moment though.

My mother would have chosen the easy route and stayed. She would have dropped everything for a new adventure such as this. In these sorts of moments, it was difficult not to think about that and compare myself to her.

I was not and never would be her. It solidified my convictions and my decision to leave to remember that. I would do what was right because that was who I was.

*****

I knew why I'd made this decision. I'd even explained it further to Tyler so he could really understand. But saying goodbye at the airport was far harder than I feared it would be.

After our bonding was complete, we had celebrated with his friends at the house. Everyone was excited for us and welcomed me with open arms, not that they had ever been anything but welcoming, but it was different, like I had somehow just inherited a family.

I knew I was going to miss all of them too.

Karis and Damon were far more settled into their bond, but she was also dealing with the distance thing as he trained for his new role as Alpha. The decision had been made and her grandparents would be stepping down after her graduation. They were confident in Karis and Damon's ability to lead the pack.

It was crazy to think about, but I was friends with a future Pack Mother. Her number was in my phone, and I had no doubt she'd take the call if I needed her.

Karis's friendship with Tyler could have put a big wedge between us, but it hadn't. Instead, we'd already begun to grow close and that was made stronger because he was so important to us both.

She still didn't approve of my leaving, but she did understand, and we had spent some time talking about what I should expect. My bond was still new and could prove even harder, but she shared some of the things they were doing to get through the weeks when he was away. I felt like I was as prepared for the three months ahead of us as possible.

With airport rules as they were, Tyler couldn't walk back and stay with me until my plane arrived. We had to say our goodbyes before I got in line to go through security. I wasn't a huge fan of flying and I waited as long as I felt comfortable to wait as we said a long and sad goodbye.

"It's not goodbye," he kept insisting. "It's just apart for now. Call me the second your plane lands."

We'd talked so much in the last twenty-four hours. I'd shared with him things I didn't think I'd ever be able to tell him, including how I had held onto that childhood promise he had made me. I told him that even once I had settled into the Virginia Pack, I couldn't fully let my guard down. I'd never dated and had distanced myself from boys, because in my heart I was his and he was going to come and get me someday.

I knew it hurt him to know that, but it was important that we talk about it. He admitted that he had forgotten about that, but he'd never forgotten about me.

It had been cleansing and necessary for me to move on.

He felt like he needed to prove to me and himself that this time things would truly be different. With our bond, I knew they would, but I'd be lying to us both if I didn't admit there was just a hint of that nagging feeling in the back of my mind that this would be the last time I saw him.

When our time was up, I hugged him, wanting to hold on forever.

He kissed me and it was hotter than should have been in public, but I didn't care, and I wasn't embarrassed by it. The rest of the world could have burned to the ground around us. I was solely focused on him.

I stared at him for one last moment memorizing his features and that feeling of completeness I got when I stared into his beautiful blue eyes.

"I'll talk to you in a few hours," I finally said, unable to formulate the word goodbye.

I forced my feet to move and bit the inside of my cheek refusing to let another tear fall. I feared if I turned around and saw him walking away that my resolve would crack.

I froze at the entrance of the line and didn't think I could go through it. I had a sick feeling in my stomach.

I chanced a look back. I didn't see his retreating back. Instead, Tyler was standing there watching me. He gave me a thumbs up for encouragement. I smiled back at him, tears were starting to cloud my eyes.

He was there, and he was supporting me every step of the way.

I lifted my head higher and took that first step and then another and another. When I rounded the first corner, I looked back again. He was still there waving me on.

I knew he didn't want me to go anymore than I wanted to leave him behind, but his presence helped show me that we were in this together and that just maybe we were going to come through it okay.

I reached the security station and presented my ID. I gave one last look back, knowing once on the other side I wouldn't be able to see him any longer.

He blew me a kiss.

I smiled and confidently walked through.

Ten minutes later I was on the other side. A moment of panic hit me hard and then my phone rang. I looked down and swiped to accept his video call.

"Your flight's showing on time and since it's a direct one you shouldn't have any problems. You better hurry though, it's already showing as boarding."

"What?" I screeched and started to run, knowing my gate was at the far end of the terminal.

"Relax, they take a while to board. You're going to be fine."

When I got there, they were just calling my group number to load onto the plane.

"I made it," I told him.

He stayed with me as I checked in and walked down to the plane to find my seat.

"All settled?"

"Yes."

"Okay, I'm going to hang up before they fuss and tell you to put your phone in airplane mode. See you in a few hours, sweetheart. I love you."

"I love you, too," I whispered.

I disconnected the call, put my phone in airplane mode, plugged in my earbuds, closed my eyes, and tried to blot out all the sadness and fears I had about leaving.

He loved me and I had to believe that it was enough to see us through.

*****

The rest of the weekend seemed to drag by, and yet, Monday morning came much too soon.

True to his word Tyler called, texted, and video chatted with me constantly. We'd even video called as I was getting ready for my first day on the job, despite the insanely early hour on the west coast.

"You should go back to sleep," I kept telling him.

"No way. It's your big day. I wasn't going to miss it. Plus, I love seeing you first thing in the morning."

"But it's not even morning there, it's the middle of the night."

"It's worth it."

I loved seeing him first thing in the morning too. Waking up alone in my tiny apartment just wasn't the same. I missed sleeping in his arms. Instead, I had pulled out Tyler Teddy and cuddled him close to me. It wasn't the same, but it did help a little. Tyler Teddy had seen me through some of my toughest times, so it was only fitting that he was there with me now. I missed Tyler so much that at times it was painful.

Wearing my new scrubs and feeling equally confident and completely unprepared, I drove over to the next town and pulled up to the hospital and parked.

It was a human hospital, but close enough to territory that we had a lot of shifters working there too. I knew I wouldn't be alone. Plus, a few of the people I had attended school with also got jobs there.

It wasn't a large area, so those jobs were highly coveted and another reason why I just couldn't give up this opportunity even if I had left my heart in California.

I entered, and then checked in at the front desk of the Emergency Department where I was going to be working. I was surprised to see a familiar face behind the counter.

"Athena? I didn't know you worked here."

Athena was one of the daughters of my Alpha. I knew who she was, but I didn't really know her. She was a few years older than me and it wasn't like I tried to make friends in the Pack. For the most part I'd kept to myself apart from them, a loner.

Being with Tyler and his friends and truly allowing myself to feel a part of something for once, made me wonder why I had been that way before. I knew deep down it was still my parents. I was a grown woman and yet a part of me was still terrified they would swoop in and take me away again.

It was hard to make connections with others with that fear hanging over me every second of my life. I made a personal vow to try and do better.

"Hey, Josie. Yeah, I've been here a few years now. Working in the ER isn't for everyone, but I love it. In fact, when I saw your name pop up, I volunteered to train you myself."

"Really?" I asked feeling a bit of relief. "Thanks."

"First day nerves?"

I considered that. Was I nervous? No. I was still torn about being here and being there with Tyler though.

"I'm not nervous."

I wasn't going to explain to her where my real nerves stemmed from. Not on my first day working with her at least.

The job was exhausting, but I loved every second of it. I thrived in the fast-paced environment, though my one regret was the lack of time for proper patient care.

After I had set Hudson's ankle back at the ARC I had spent days fussing over him and caring for him. I was surprised by how good that felt. I needed that extra time and compassion more than I realized.

I had chosen the ER as my first choice because I thought I didn't want that part of the job. I didn't want to really care, and I knew I was efficient and effective. I never considered that wouldn't be enough for me.

Athena was a great teacher, and she clearly loved the job. I enjoyed working with her, but when it was time to clock out, I walked away without a second thought.

On my drive home, I called Tyler.

"Hey, how did it go?" he asked, answering on the first ring.

I didn't know why, but I always got this second of panic when I called him as if he wasn't going to answer the phone or I had somehow imagined it all. As soon as I heard his voice, that fear disappeared.

"It was okay. I'm pretty tired. It was a long day."

"Are you okay?"

"Yeah, I'm great." I was overexaggerating it so not to make him feel guilty. How could I ever be great without him?

"Well, tell me all about it."

"My trainer will most likely be my supervisor too. She's Pack so that's nice. Actually, Athena is Daniel's daughter."

"Your Alpha?"

"Yes."

"I spoke with him again today to officially let him know we bonded."

"You did?"

"Well, just in case I can't handle things and need to see you, I wanted him aware of the situation and ensured I had his permission to enter his territory and all."

My chest warmed and I couldn't stop smiling. I didn't want him to suffer, but it was nice to know it was hard for him too.

We stayed on the phone talking as we walked through our evening right up until I couldn't stop yawning and was struggling to keep my eyes opened.

Tyler laughed. "Get some sleep, Josie. I'll talk to you tomorrow."

"Okay, but not in the morning. I need you to get sleep too. We'll be fine for twenty-four hours."

He hesitated. "Okay, I can try it."

"I miss you."

"Miss you, too, sweetheart. Have a great day tomorrow."

"You, too."

"I love you."

"Love you, too," I managed through a yawn.

He chuckled. "Sweet dreams."

I hated hearing the silence that followed. I grabbed Tyler Teddy for comfort, but I was so exhausted that by the time my head hit my pillow, I was out.

*****

I was grumpy the next morning and regretted telling Tyler to sleep instead of calling me first thing in the morning. Selfishly, I wished he had anyway, but I knew he needed his sleep too.

When I got to the hospital, I was not my usual chipper self and I suppose it showed.

"Office, now," Athena ordered the second she saw me.

I groaned. I had no idea what I had done to piss her off, but it was not the way I wanted to start my second day on the job.

She closed the door behind and then turned to me. She scowled before throwing her arms around my neck.

I froze. I didn't know how to respond.

"Are you okay?" she asked.

"Um, yeah. I'm not late am I?"

She laughed releasing me.

I took a step back from her.

"I was at my parents' house for dinner last night and I heard the news. I guess you didn't mean to share it, but a true mate? Wow! Josie, that's huge. How are you holding up? Dad said he's back in California."

I sighed sadly. "I'm okay. We'll get through it. It's only three months."

"Are you sure?"

I nodded. "I worked really hard for this job, Athena. I need to be here, and he graduates in three months and needs to be there. It sucks, but we're going to get through it."

"Mom said you were only gone a week. That's not exactly time to really get to know someone and seal a bond? You're a lot braver than I am."

"Tyler and I knew each other as kids. To be honest, I've been in love with him since I was four years old."

"Oh my gosh! Are you serious? That's amazing," she gushed. "So did you already know you were true mates?"

"No. I hadn't seen him in fifteen years."

Her eyes widened. "So you reconnected with him? That's so sweet."

I grinned. "He's the best."

"Aw, you literally light up talking about him."

She hugged me again. "I really don't comprehend the whole true mate thing. My brother Jeremy dated his mate, Amy, all through college. They decided to apply for compatible mating and got approved. He chose well and they are very happy. That makes sense to me. It's a lot like humans… fall in love, know you're compatible, the request for approval is sort of like an engagement period, and then bonded. But I am so fascinated by true mates."

She acted like I didn't know who her brother and his mate were. They were the Alpha heir and future Pack Mother of the Virginia Pack. Of course, I knew who they were.

"Amber's planning to take a compatible mate too. He's a great guy and they are a solid match. There's nothing wrong with that plan."

"But true mates just seem like something more," she said wistfully. "My brother Gage found his true mate. Clara's the best and they are so happy together. Sometimes it's like they can't even keep their hands off each other. They do everything together and never seem to want to be apart."

I sighed. "I know how that feels."

"See, I'm convinced there's just something extra about true mates." She frowned. "I've had a few mating offers. It could be a smart match, but then I see this almost otherworldly look in your eyes when you mention your mate. What was his name?"

"Tyler."

"See, there it is. I want that. I don't want to settle for a compatible mate. Is that bad?"

I shook my head no in understanding. "Having experienced it now, I struggle to understand how anyone could settle for less."

She hugged me once more. "Thank you, Josie. I really needed that affirmation right now." She took a deep breath and straightened her scrubs. "On that note, we should probably get to work."

"Does it include coffee? I didn't sleep well last night," I admitted.

"That can be arranged."

*****

Work was just work. I liked it just fine, but it was nowhere as fulfilling as I had somehow imagined it. Everything moved at such a fast pace that I really didn't have time to make any real connections with my patients and by Friday they were already starting to just become a blur of numbers and descriptions… the old guy in bed four, gunshot awaiting OR, or the kid in three.

Shortly after lunch, Athena pulled me into the office once more.

"How are you holding up?"

I didn't want to admit that I resented the job and feared I'd made a huge mistake ever leaving California. I had been so focused on not being like my mother that I had stubbornly given up my own happiness in the hopes of doing the right and responsible thing.

Maybe it was the responsible thing to do, but it sure didn't feel like the right thing for me.

"Everything's fine," I said before beginning a rundown on my current patient stats.

"No, Josie, how are you, not your patients, *you*?"

I sighed. "It's a little harder than I had expected, being away from Tyler, but I'm managing. It's only three months. We're going to get through this. I don't think it's affecting my job any."

"No, it's not. You're quite efficient and you are excellent with the patients. You're a really great nurse, Josie, but I also sense that the Emergency Department isn't right for you."

"What? What did I do wrong? Just tell me, Athena. I can fix it, I promise."

"Relax, Josie. Take a deep breath. I'm not firing you. I'm just saying that I think you need to reassess your options."

"I don't have a backup plan. This is it for me. I have to make this work."

"Well that is where you are very wrong. I've been watching you and you thrive in patient care. I wish you could see yourself when you have more than five seconds with a patient. You are such a comfort to them and you really know how to connect with people."

"I do?" I asked. I'd never really felt like I connected with anyone in life—except Tyler.

"You do. You are so good with people, too good for this place. I like the disconnect the ER gives us, but I fear it's going to squash all your goodness here. So I spoke to my dad about it."

My face felt like it was on fire. "You told the Alpha I wasn't good at my job?"

She laughed at my horrified expression. "It wasn't like that, Josie. Quite the opposite really. I explained you were too good at your job."

"What does that mean?"

"Do you know Simon?"

"The Pack physician?"

"Yes."

"Of course."

"I didn't want to assume, but I figured. So Simon has been begging for some time off and flexibility. He's single and fears he's never going to find a mate while stuck in the clinic day in and day out. He wants a few months off this summer and that means the Pack has to fill in with a new position, or at least a temporary one."

"Okay?"

"Dad's been consulting with me on this, and I know he wants me to take it on. We aren't looking for another doctor, but a nurse with exceptional care and able to connect well with people. It's a small town, but you already know that. Hiring from within the Pack would be ideal. Dad's under the assumption from talks with your mate that he hopes to move here and pledge his allegiance after graduation, is that right?"

I nodded. "Yes. He knows I don't want to leave the Pack and he doesn't really want to go back to New York City."

"Great, so I suggested, rather strongly, that you be given the position."

"What? Me? But that's a Pack position and I trained on humans, plus, I need a permanent position, not a possible temporary one."

"We're all aware of that, but apparently you failed to mention healing a certain football star during your time at the ARC."

"Hudson. He broke his ankle dancing if you can believe that. I suspect it was in about three places, but with the storm and power outages I didn't have resources to verify that. I've worked just a little with Simon in the past and he taught me a couple of things. It was just sheer luck that it worked out."

"Josie, Hudson is fully healed and has full mobility of his ankle. His coach personally called to sing your praises, and he wants you on his staff back at the ARC. Before you freak out and tell me no, just hear me out. You would fly back to California and work on the physical therapy team there for the sports department until mid-May. Then you would fly back here to train alongside Simon who feels your particular skills that you'll gain at the ARC will come in handy as his assistant here. There is a catch though."

"What?" I asked, not certain yet how I felt about any of this.

"There's a two year commitment with the sports department at the ARC, but you will have summer and winter breaks off. Simon will expect you to help cover for him and work with him during those periods with the guarantee that after two years, should you decide to return home, you will be given a permanent job as his assistant and the official Pack nurse."

I blew out a long breath. "That's a lot."

"It really is, and as much as I hate the thought of losing you around here, you really need to consider this offer, Josie. It's a great opportunity for you in areas where you can truly flourish."

I nodded. "I'll do it," I said, shocking us both.

It was the most spontaneous thing I'd ever agreed to in my entire life.

"Are you sure?"

"Yes, and if I can fly out this weekend, even better."

"You miss him that much?"

Tears filled my eyes as I nodded. "I don't want to be away from him, Athena."

She smiled and then pulled me to her for a hug.

"I'm going to clock us both out and we'll go talk to Dad and Simon, okay?"

I nodded feeling this enormous weight lifted from my chest.

I could do this. I had a plan, and it was a good one. I wasn't going to ruin my life just because I chose to follow my heart.

Tyler

Chapter 25

The second my last class ended on Thursday, I headed over to catch both of my professors for my Friday classes. I needed to explain to them my upcoming absence and turn in a few assignments. Much to my relief, neither of them cared that I was ditching out on their classes tomorrow.

On my way out, my advisor called me into his office.

"How are you doing, Tyler?"

"Um, good."

"I know the last we talked you had said you weren't really interested in sticking around for your masters. Is that still the case? Or have you changed your mind?"

"I haven't changed my mind."

"Are you sure?" he asked as he handed an envelope to me. "Because this is an offer and invitation."

"I never even took the test."

"Every one of your professors vouched for you. It's a full scholarship for two more years. Think about it."

I didn't know what to say. I had been adamant that I didn't want this, but it was a huge opportunity that was hard to just walk away from.

"I took a mate," I blurted out.

He seemed a little surprised to hear it. "Congratulations. Of course there is always mated housing as an option."

"But she lives and works in Virginia."

"I see. That definitely complicates things."

"I have to do what's best for the both of us now."

"You know what. Take it, look it over, and talk to her. I do understand and appreciate your dilemma, but I'd hate for you to just toss away such a big honor here."

I didn't want to take the envelope. I didn't want to think about it. I wasn't sure I was going to make it through to graduation but for certain I couldn't survive two more years separated from my mate.

I didn't tell him that though. Instead, I took it and thanked him.

Once outside, I stuffed it into my backpack and practically skipped all the way back to the doghouse, shut myself into my room, and started making plans.

I'd survived five whole days without my girl, but I'd be damned if I was going to let another one pass me by.

There was a knock at my door.

"It's open," I yelled.

Pete poked his head in. "Hey, oh, are you leaving?"

"Got an early flight in the morning, so I'm going to crash at one of the airport hotels tonight. Brian said he'd drive me over. Want to ride along?"

"Um," he looked at his watch and frowned. "Can't. Sorry."

"What's going on with you, man?"

"Nothing," he said a little too fast. I knew something was up with him this semester as he was acting weirder than usual and keeping to himself a lot.

"Come on Pete. I worry about you."

"There's nothing to worry about. I'm fine. And I'm glad you're going to see Josie. That is where you're going, right?"

I chuckled. "Absolutely."

He grinned. "I like her. She's really good for you."

"Thanks. I like her too."

He stood around for a few minutes and I had the feeling he wanted to talk.

"Well, I'll let you go. Tell Josie hi."

"Pete, are you sure you don't want to talk? I'm not in any rush to get to the airport."

For a moment I thought he was going to finally open up to me about whatever's been going on with him, but instead he just shook his head and smiled.

"It's all good. Have a great trip. Will you be back next week."

"Probably," I said evasively.

The truth was I didn't know what the hell I was going to do yet. I still firmly understood the need for me to get my diploma, but at what cost?

One day at a time, I reminded myself.

Step by step we'd get through it and my first step was to pack and be on that plane at four in the morning. I was going to surprise my girl.

*****

The flight was direct to Washington, DC. From there I had to rent a car and it was a couple hours to my destination. I cranked up the music and tried to keep my speed within an appropriate range that wouldn't get me stopped by a cop.

I wanted to get there quickly, and I certainly didn't need to add the additional time for a speeding ticket.

As I pulled up in front of the apartment, I could feel myself begin to relax. That was until I walked up to her door and knocked and was greeted with silence.

I looked down at my watch and frowned. It felt so much later, but it was only two-thirty and I knew she wouldn't even get off of work until three.

I didn't have a key to her place, and I didn't know the territory to go poking around. That's when it dawned on me that I hadn't warned Daniel I was coming.

I cringed and quickly dialed his number.

"Hello?"

"Alpha Daniel?"

"Tyler Klein? What can I do for you, son?"

"I just wanted to give you a heads up that I'm here."

"Here? In my territory?"

"Yes, sir. You did say it was okay anytime."

"I did, and to be honest I'm a little surprised you lasted this long. When I hadn't heard from you in the last forty-eight hours, I thought perhaps things were settling down some." He chuckled.

I cringed. Had I really been that bad?

"Sorry sir. I just, I just couldn't take it any longer. I had to come and see her."

"She doesn't know you're here, does she?"

"No," I confessed.

"Well, she left my office about ten minutes ago. If she went straight home, she should be pulling up any second now."

"Wait, she wasn't at work? Why was she in your office? Is everything okay? Alpha, is my mate okay?"

I could hear the smile in his voice. "Simmer down. She's fine, but I'm going to let her explain it all. And yes, Tyler, you are always welcome here."

"Thanks, sir," I mumbled suddenly more concerned with why Josie was skipping work to meet with her Alpha.

Every time a car pulled up, I jumped up expecting to see her. After another fifteen minutes of that, I started to pace, worried something bad had happened.

Finally, I forced myself to sit down. I closed my eyes and tried to let go of my fears. It wasn't working, but it made me feel like I was doing something.

I heard another car pull up, but I didn't react or even open my eyes, I just stayed focused on remaining calm and convincing myself not to put Daniel's information in my GPS and trace the route she likely took from there.

I had never been the best tracker, but I had a certain advantage when it came to Josie.

"Tyler?" my eyes popped open as she reached the top step.

I jumped up and ran to her pulling her into my arms and kissing her breathless.

She laughed and slowed my advances. It was probably a good thing. I probably would have taken her right there for the whole apartment complex to witness.

I shuddered letting her touch sooth and calm me.

She placed her palm against my cheek and looked up at me with dreamy eyes like she wasn't quite sure if I was really here or not.

"What are you doing here?"

I was a little ashamed to admit it, but then this was Josie and I knew she would forgive me.

"I couldn't stand to be away from you a second longer."

"But you have classes today."

"I know. I cleared it with my professors first. It's okay. I just," I paused, trying to gather my thoughts. "I know I said I was handling everything okay, but I'm not. I miss you so much it physically hurts."

Her arms wrapped tighter around me. "I miss you too."

"Where were you?" I looked down at my watch. More than half an hour had passed. "Daniel said you weren't at work and left his office over forty minutes ago."

"You spoke with Daniel again?"

I shrugged. "I wanted to warn him I was here."

She laughed. "He told me of all the wolves he's responsible for, he spends more time talking with my mate than anyone else these days."

I groaned. "He hates me already?"

"No, he was actually very pleased about it."

"So why were you there and not work?"

She grinned and shook her head. "Come on in and I'll tell you all about it."

We didn't talk right away though. The second the door closed I was freeing her from her scrubs before making love to her right on her small kitchen table. I couldn't help myself. I had to have her.

She giggled, looking sated. "Better?" she teased me.

"I missed you," I frowned.

She sat up and kissed my frown away.

"I think we should talk. A lot has happened this week and I'd like your opinion on some things."

A bad feeling was sinking into the pit of my stomach, yet I felt no nerves or concern coming from her.

"Okay," I said.

I couldn't help but think of the offer to grad school still sitting in my backpack. I hadn't even opened up. Should I tell her about that? No, I decided. I didn't want her to feel any guilt for staying here. I had promised her we'd only be apart three months, and I was going to keep that promise. I would start job hunting soon, maybe even put out some feelers while I was in town.

"Tyler, are you even listening?"

"What? Yeah, of course."

"I just told you I want to move to the ARC and you didn't even flinch in the least."

"Sure, the ARC. You want to.... Wait, what?

She laughed. "I knew you weren't listening."

"Don't tease me like that. I promise, you have my full attention now. What did you really want to talk to me about?"

"I wouldn't joke about something like that. There's a catch though."

"What are we talking about?"

"Do I need to put clothes on to get you to pay attention?"

"Probably," I confessed, even knowing that hadn't been my distraction for once.

"Tyler, I don't know if I can handle three months apart and with Daniel and Athena's help, I have a new job offer. It's at the ARC. I'd be working with the sports department. Apparently, Hudson's coaches were very impressed with his ankle when he explained to them what happened. They offered me a fulltime position there. After graduation I would come back here and assist Simon, our Pack physician with the Pack clinic. It's a good offer, really good actually."

"So what's the catch?" I asked.

She bit her bottom lip and then looked me in the eyes. "They want a two year commitment."

"What about the clinic here?" I asked trying desperately not to get my hopes up.

"Simon was in the meeting with Daniel as we hashed everything out. I'd spend the next few summer and winter breaks here shadowing him and learning the ropes with a guaranteed position of Pack nurse when I complete the two years requirement at the ARC. But you're graduating in just three months so it doesn't even make sense to be discussing this, right?"

"Are you sure this is what you want, Josie?"

"What I want is to be with you, Tyler. I thought it mattered, that somehow if I chose you above all else that I would be no different than my parents, but I'm not them, Tyler. I'm not the girl who can pack up and leave everything behind without a second glance, but I'm ready to go back with you. I can just take sabbatical for three months. Athena says I can always come back to the hospital, so I'm not shutting any doors."

"But you really are interested in this position at the ARC?" I asked. I had to know that this is what she truly wanted and not what she thought I'd want for her.

"I felt needed when I was helping Hudson, I got to care for him, and see him through from the start of his injury until he was fully healed. The ER is fine, but it's so impersonal and turns out, this little loner is actually really great with people. Who knew? If I can do that sort of work fulltime, then yes, that's what I want. But it's not just me anymore, Tyler. And it's not fair for me to ask you to stick around just for me."

I shrugged. "Damon's done it for three years for Karis."

"And that's fine for them, but what would you do there?"

I couldn't hold my grin back any longer. "I got into grad school. I didn't even apply, but some of my professors put me up for consideration anyway. I just found out last night. My advisor says it's a full ride and everything. Two years, Josie. They want me to stick around for two more years."

"And is that something you want?"

"I didn't think I did, but I would be lying if I wasn't excited for the opportunity. I haven't even been able to make myself open the envelope, like it's Pandora's box or something and could alter my path forever if I even peek at it. But if you want to be at the ARC working the next two years, then…"

"You could finish your master's."

"Yes."

She threw her arms around me and squealed.

"You aren't just doing this for me, are you?"

"No, but always yes."

"Same. I think we should take this, Tyler. It can't be a coincidence that all of this is coming together right now."

"No, it's fate," I insisted. I looked around her apartment. "What will we do with all your stuff here?"

"Funny you should ask. The reason I took so long to get home is because I stopped by Aunt Courtney's on the way. I told her everything, including about you and all my fears of turning out like my mother. She really helped me finally realize that I am not my parents, and I never will be. I've been coming to that realization slowly on my own, but hearing it validated from her really helped. And she said I could store anything I had at her place. If we get packing and move everything over tomorrow, we could probably get flights out for Sunday and be home before you have to go to class on Monday."

"Home?" I asked.

"Home."

"You really think you'll be okay calling the ARC home for the next few years?"

She shook her head. "No, I'll be calling wherever you are home from now on."

Josie

Epilogue

"Pollock, what the hell did you do this time?" I asked as I rushed into the small clinic I had carved out for myself in a corner of the rehab center. It was a place I could see patients with a slight bit of privacy. At first it had been a curtain, and then some recycled partitions on wheels, but just recently, Coach Jacobs had real walls installed for me.

Damon had even given me a dampener in celebration of my new office and now my patients could speak freely without the threat of shifter ears listening in to every little thing.

"Sorry doc. Thanks for coming in on the weekend."

"I got your 911 text. I'm here. Now tell me why?"

Pollock was usually one of the good guys. I'd had problems with a few and had to put my foot down with them. I was young and despite public knowledge that I was mated, it didn't stop the guys from hitting on me.

Over the last few months I'd had a few of these emergency calls only to be put in a compromised position with a determined young man trying to see how far he could press my patience.

That was mostly in the early days. I had firmly held my ground and drawn that line with them and I didn't really think any of them would try and cross it again, at least not until the new freshman batch arrived in the fall.

Hudson had helped a lot with my transition and I credited him to the fact I'd only had a couple of these incidents, but it had been enough that I cringed every time one of these texts came in.

It also set Tyler's wolf on edge which was why he was sitting just outside my office, waiting. I had watched him stare Pollock down as he walked in. Now that the guys knew my mate, no one wanted to cross him.

Tyler was the sweetest most easy-going man in the world, until someone messed with me, then he was downright scary.

"I think I pulled my hamstring," Pollock finally told me. "I can't even fully stretch my leg right now."

"Hop up on the table. Let me take a look."

I felt his injury and noticed his muscle was truly tight, really tight. I massaged it out as he cried out in pain.

I wanted to groan in frustration. Pollock was a dual athlete. He played baseball in the spring and football in the fall. Coach was not going to be happy about this if I couldn't get that muscle to release.

Most shifters rarely required over the counter human meds, but I took a chance with this and gave him a handful of ibuprofen. Our metabolisms were much higher than humans so we require more of the drugs.

"Aw, doc, I hate these things."

"Do you want this muscle to relax so you can play this week or not?"

He sighed and took the pills.

No matter how many times I tried to tell them that I wasn't actually a doctor, I was just a nurse, they insisted on calling me doc anyway. It was kind of endearing and felt like they had accepted me into their pack when they issued the nickname. I no longer bothered to even try to correct them anymore.

I opened the door to let Tyler know everything was okay. He wrapped me up in his arms and kissed me.

"No PDA, doc. Your rules, remember?" Pollock yelled out.

I shook my head. "I also don't work off hours, remember?" I dished back.

He chuckled. "Touché."

Fifteen minutes later I checked on him again. At least I could actually move the muscle some now. I straightened his leg slowly, happy to see some of the tension had already lifted.

Tyler sat in the corner, distracting my patient as I got to work rubbing out the kinks in Pollock' leg. It wasn't glamorous work by any means. Sprains and strains were my new expertise and I considering taking some massage therapy classes over summer break as that seemed to be a necessary part of this job.

Working with the various teams at the ARC had proven to be far more rewarding than I could ever have imagined.

Athena had been right about me. I did thrive in patient care. I liked knowing my patients, sometimes a bit too well, but overall, I knew I was truly making a difference here and helping these athletes. That was really why I had chosen nursing to begin with.

"Okay. I think that's good for now. When's your next game?" I asked as if I didn't have every team's schedule memorized already.

"Wednesday."

"I want you to hit the hot tub for a bit and then head home. And don't even think about calling in your friends this time. No parties in my rehab center. Are we clear?"

He gave me a sheepish grin. "Yes ma'am."

"I want to see you tomorrow for a follow-up. What's your class schedule look like?"

"Oh, well, I can come at anytime that works for you."

Tyler snorted. "Does that really work?"

Pollock grinned again and shrugged. "Worth a try."

"I can look it up in your file if I have to."

He huffed. "I have classes from eleven to four."

"Okay, let's do first thing in the morning then. How about nine?"

"Doc, that's so early," he whined.

"I could make it eight?" I gave him a sweet smile.

"Nine's fine." He scowled at me.

"Stay off that leg as much as possible. If you aren't willing to do that then I'll get the crutches and if you don't rest it properly and I don't see improvement tomorrow, then you know what comes next."

"Not the chair," he complained.

I bit back a smile. I hadn't had to actually use the wheelchair, but I did have two of them lined up in plain sight and used them as threats often. It always worked to get them to behave and actually abide by my instructions with minimal complaint.

It hadn't been easy to earn their respect or to get them to fear me enough to listen, but I was over that hurdle now and couldn't be happier with my life.

Pollock limped over to the hot tub, shred the last of his clothes, and climbed in with a sigh. I knew he was happy not to be getting an ice bath, but I had a feeling that could be necessary in the morning.

"All in a day's work," Tyler teased as he wrapped his arms around my waist while I scrubbed down the table.

He kissed my shoulder.

I had never felt more content with life. My fears of leaving my life behind in Virginia and following Tyler to California had long since been laid to rest. He would be graduating in two weeks, and we'd be heading back to Virginia for the summer.

I was looking forward to returning in August though. Tyler would be starting graduate school, instead of mated housing we decided to stay in the doghouse at least for the next year. We had our own space and it just felt like home.

That's all I'd ever truly wanted—a home.

Though I hated to admit it, I finally understood what my mother had meant all those years of bouncing us from place to place. I still couldn't handle her freestyle life, but I could accept it a little better now.

She'd always told me that home wasn't a place it was the people you loved most and as long as you had that, you had everything.

I had thought I needed more. I had always wanted to put down roots, a pack to call my own, and a physical place to call home. In a way, I had all those things now, but more importantly, I had Tyler. He was my home, and I knew that no matter what life threw our way or where it took us, as long as he was by my side, I was grounded and safe. I was home.

*****

If you enjoyed Josie & Tyler's story, check out Karis & Damon in Pack's Promise.

Or, if you are new to my PNR world, go back to the book that started it all with Kyle & Kelsey's story in One True Mate.

And if you are a Kindle Unlimited reader, you're in luck! ALL of my books are currently enrolled in KU, so prepare to binge!

Dear Reader,

Thanks for reading Forgotten Promise. If you enjoyed Tyler and Josie's story, please consider dropping a review. https://mybook.to/ARC8 It helps more than you know.

For further information on my books, events, and life in general, I can be found online here:

Website: www.julietrettel.com

Facebook

Instagram

Bookbub

Goodreads

Amazon

Sign up for my Newsletter with a free Westin Pack Short Story!

Love my books?
Join my Reader Group, Julie Trettel's Book Lover's!

With love and thanks,
Julie Trettel

Sneak Peek

HIDDEN PROMISE

ARC Shifters

Coming May 12, 2022

*****

I stared at myself in the mirror unable to believe what I was seeing. The dress was everything, even more perfect than I imagined it would be when I first saw it in the store window.

I took a step back and twirled.

"Perfect!"

I carefully applied my makeup and pulled my hair up into a bun.

Knock. Knock. Knock.

"Dad I'm almost ready. Two more minutes."

"Okay, okay. I'm just nervous, Sadie."

I laughed. "It's my prom, Dad. What on Earth do you have to be nervous about?"

I opened the door and stepped out. His eyes glassed over with unshed tears.

"Oh honey, you look absolutely stunning. How I wish your mother was here to see you now."

I grinned. "She's here, Dad. She's always here."

"I know she is. I see her every single day right there in your eyes."

"Love you, Dad."

"I love you too, honey. And you're going to have the night of your life tonight, but not too much fun."

I laughed. "Wouldn't dream of it."

I had the perfect dress, the perfect date, and a prom queen crown by the end of the night, but all of that faded into the background when a new reality set in.

For eighteen years I was an average, or maybe slightly above average, human being, and suddenly, I wasn't human at all.

My senior prom should have been the greatest night of my life up until that point of it at least, and for a while, it was. After my date and I were crowned as Prom King and Queen, my skin started itching. It got really bad. I couldn't see the hives, but I could feel them. It was so bad I had to call it an early night and go home in search of Benadryl.

I didn't make it home that night to take it though. Instead, I shifted into a big scary wolf right in my front yard seconds after my date drove out of sight.

My beautiful dress laid in shreds across my front lawn. I was alone and I was terrified.

I hid under the porch for two days.

I had no idea what to do or where to go.

Somehow, my father knew, though. That hurt more than anything. He had known I was a monster because he was one too, and yet, he had never bothered to explain things to me.

*****

And check out these great books by Julie Trettel!

Westin Pack

One True Mate
Fighting Destiny
Forever Mine
Confusing Hearts
Can't Be Love
Under a Harvest Moon

Collier Pack

Breathe Again
Run Free
In Plain Sight
Broken Chains
Coming Home
Holiday Surprise

ARC Shifters

Pack's Promise
Winter's Promise
Midnight Promise
iPromise
New Promise
Don't Promise
Protected Promise

Westin Force

Fierce Impact
Rising Storm
Collision Course
Technical Threat
Final Extraction
Waging War

Bonus Westin World Books

The Diner 2

A Collier First Christmas

Shifter Marked and Claimed

Julie also writes these All Ages Series
Check out more great books by Jules Trettel!

Armstrong Academy

Louis and the Secrets of the Ring
Octavia and the Tiny Tornadoes
William and the Look Alike
Hannah and the Sea of Tears
Eamon and the Mysteries of Magic
May and the Strawberry Scented Catastrophe
Gil and the Hidden Tunnels
Elaina and the History of Helios
Alaric and the Shaky Start
Mack and the Disappearing Act
Halloween and the Secret's Blown
Ivan and the Masked Crusader

Stones of Amaria

Legends of Sorcery
Ruins of Magic
Keeper of Light
Fall of Darkness

The Compounders Series

The Compounders: Book1
DISSENSION
DISCONTENT
SEDITION

About the Author

Julie Trettel is a USA Today Bestselling Author of Paranormal Romance. She comes from a long line of story tellers. Writing has always been a stress reliever and escape for her to manage the crazy demands of juggling time and schedules between work and an active family of six. In her "free time," she enjoys traveling, reading, outdoor activities, and spending time with family and friends.

Visit

www.JulieTrettel.com